QUIRKY BLACK SCI-FI
TALES

By

M'Shai S. Dash

Acknowledgments

These stories would still be in a forgotten folder on my laptop without the encouragement, words of wisdom, and overall support I received from my family and friends. It's impossible to dole out all the gratitude I feel towards them for their hand in this, but I'd especially like to thank Tiara, Mujadala, Shaykh, Ma, Daddy, Robert, Maurice, and the immensely talented community of writers who showed me that it's possible to push things out into the world, even in the midst of a pandemic. I'm grateful for this project and the time the universe granted me to finish it. Most of all, I'm grateful for the understanding I gained during this time and eager to interpret the world differently because of it. My time here is a gift, togetherness is a privilege, and gratitude for both is a discipline all its own. Thank you all.

Contents

The Braided One

Emma rolled over from a blissful sleep and instinctively reached for Anthony, but her hand landed on a disheveled array of pillows and turned back sheets instead. She reached for her phone on the nightstand. The burgeoning golds that marked a sunrise halfway done let her know that it was nearly six before she confirmed. The blades of light filtered through the almost closed blinds in her bedroom, mincing the last of the darkness away and prompting her to rise. She sat up and listened for sounds from the bathroom. Then, she checked her phone again.

No text to tell me he was leaving out early, either. Emma swung her feet over the bed and let her feet find the furry insides of her slippers but remained sitting on the bed a while longer, fuming to herself. *That was the least he could do. He really is triflin'.*

She leaned forward at the waist to let her braids cascade forward from the nape of her neck before securing it atop her head with a sturdy tie. Then, she stood and wound them into a high bun that advanced her height from a petite 5'1 to nearly

5'5.

"Why do you get 'em so long, girl? Aren't they heavy?" Emma's friend Tanya once remarked after she noticed that the lengthy braids had become her signature style.

"Iont know," Emma shrugged. "Maybe I do it for the same reason some women wear heels all the time—I wanna stand out. Sometimes people need a reason to look at you before they're willing to listen to you, I guess. Plus, they're just easier to deal with."

As she passed her dresser on her way to the bathroom, she glanced at the framed pictures of her and her friends. In one, she and a longtime friend, Natasha, stood smiling in shimmery slip dresses and tall heels at a resort restaurant in Negril, Jamaica. Nearly the same in height and color, people often mistook them for sisters. They also shared the same love of reading, science fiction, and poetry.

Emma picked up the next framed photo and studied it for a moment. In this one, she was with Tanya, posed with their backsides to the camera as they looked over their shoulders. Emma wore a form-fitting backless dress that night, and as risqué as it had felt when she put it on, she still felt it looked conservative next to Tanya, who had donned barely-there shorts for the occasion. Natasha had moved to the west coast for work, but Tanya had remained in Emma's area. Though they saw each other often, Emma soon realized that

Natasha had been the common denominator that balanced their two personalities. She placed the old photo back on the dresser.

Ha, Emma mused as she shuffled lazily to the bathroom. *None of us look quite like that anymore. I should replace them with some recent pics from my phone.*

Emma showered, dressed, then carefully applied her makeup and let her braids down. She looked at herself in the bathroom mirror and thought again of the pictures and Anthony, who had been leaving earlier and earlier when he spent the night, and seldom took her out anymore. The thunderstorm during the previous evening made for a cozy date night in, so she hadn't complained. They'd ordered in, watched their favorite shows, and let things progress as they always did.

Something's different with him, Emma frowned into the mirror, and the same small-faced, honey-colored woman with big, discerning eyes frowned back as she always had. *Or...maybe I shouldn't overthink it. It's been three months, and that's pretty solid, I guess. Does it matter that we don't go out as much anymore? Is that such a big deal?*

Still, she surveyed her face carefully. Faint crow's feet had begun to bloom from the outer corners of her eyes, and the athletic build she'd maintained throughout college had softened and widened with the years. She welcomed the weight gain since she'd always felt her body was akin to a minimalist chair while Tanya's was like a plush, velvet couch.

Emma's phone chimed, and she rushed from the bathroom to grab it, snatching it off of the disheveled bed. Her eyes scanned the notifications, looking for Anthony's text. But it was Tanya.

"Stranded," the text from Tanya began. "Mad as fuck at this bitch ass nigga. Please send me $40, so I can get home. Hate to ask. Got you back Friday, though."

Emma stared at the text, swallowed hard, then sent the money. A few moments went by, so she texted her back "sent" and awaited a response. None came.

Really?! Not even a 'thank you'? This is the third time in two months. How does she keep getting herself into this mess?

Emma cruised through most of the morning's perfunctory tasks on autopilot. At the same time, her thoughts flitted between Anthony's growing indifference and Tanya's casual dependence on her to bail her out of her foiled escapades. She mumbled to herself as she jammed a single-serve coffee pod into her brewing machine and slammed her pans around on the stove while cooked breakfast. By the time she carried her steaming mug to the table and opened her laptop for the day, she had barely calmed down.

After a pandemic shut the doors of her IT firm for over a year, Emma was elated to find that some of the remote-work policies stuck long afterward. The company had restructured its telework agreements, and Emma eventually became accustomed to working in solitude from home. Only one coworker had been a thorn in her side throughout the transition; Nathan.

At least I haven't heard much from him today, Emma thought as she stood up and stretched. *I think I'll grab a few things from the store before lunch.*

Another thing that Emma loved about working from home was the ability to start work early, then take breaks as she pleased. She used to love when Anthony would get off early from his construction gigs and come over in the afternoon. They'd cut out for lunch or spend the afternoon entrenched in each other the entire time. They'd made love in nearly every part of the house back then. One time, they had a picnic in the backyard, and Emma straddled him, moaning until the dogs next door began to bark aggressively near the fence.

It's so hard to stay mad at him. Emma sighed and glanced at her phone. *Still no text, though. I hate this shit!*

She grabbed her keys and left for the store. As she climbed into her truck, a guy on her block catcalled her. She shot him an evil look over her shoulder before slamming her door and pulling off.

"Is that all for today?" Gerald asked from behind the counter, smiling his usual smile.

"That's all," Emma nodded as she spoke, trying to decide—as she did every visit—if the oddness of Gerald's grin was caused by him having too many teeth or if too many of his teeth were simply the wrong size.

"I like those braids on you—you just get 'em done?" Gerald oozed the words out, and Emma noticed that he bagged each item excruciatingly slow as he did.

"Yeah," Emma forced a smile. "Last weekend."

"They look nice," Gerald pushed for the up-sale with an even wider grin.

Here he goes. Emma struggled to keep her eyes from rolling and concentrated on controlling her expression overall. *Can't I grab my shit without all this small talk? Never fails.*

"We've got a new brand of wine in," Gerald informed her in a tone that was practically hymnal. "Perfect day to try some."

"Not today," Emma tapped her foot impatiently. It was the one gesture of frustration she knew Gerald couldn't spot from behind the counter. "And I've really gotta get going. Still on the clock."

"Right," he handed her card back wrapped neatly in a receipt, and Emma moved toward the door, grateful that he didn't engage any further and make her late.

Emma saw that an older woman was close behind her, waddling forward with a handful of bags and a determined look on her face. Her red hair was in tight curls, and her cheeks were flushed beet-colored from her efforts. Emma looked at her car longingly. It was only a few dozen feet away. Then, she looked back at the woman, who was quickly closing the distance between herself and the exit of the old convenience store. Defeated, Emma sighed, shifted her bags to the other arm, and held the door for the winded woman. She waited a moment for the woman to give her a nod over the shoulder or huff out a breathy word of appreciation, but instead, she shrank slowly in the distance without offering any form of 'thank you' at all.

Emma scoffed, let out a long, shaky breath, then flung her bags on the back seat and climbed into the driver's seat of her small SUV, taking care not to sit on her braids as she often did when she was in a hurry.

So much for manners. Emma sighed and pushed the ignition button. *At least I got outta there in time to fix a snack before this boring conference meeting.*

The car on her left swerved in front of her without cutting its turning signal on, then sat in the turning lane, idling. Watching the green arrow switch to red, Emma felt a bout of rage whip itself into a cyclone inside of her.

"Ugh," Emma grunted, then cursed under her breath the whole way home.

As she exited her car, she noticed that her lawn was freshly cut.

This day's not a total loss, she thought as she looked it over approvingly.

Emma hung her keys on the hook near her front door, tossed her bag onto the sofa, and kicked off her shoes before journeying deeper into her home. Her waist-length braids swayed behind her hips as she walked, keeping rhythm with the swing of her arms and hips. As she passed the large leaner mirror in the corner of her living room, she peered at her reflection and was again pleased to see how well the braids complimented her high cheekbones. Emma loved everything about the style, including the wispy hairs she'd sculpted into intricate swirls that framed her face.

She tended to the plants on each windowsill as she passed from the small, colorful living room into the bright dining room, which was home to more plants in its corners, but no dining room table. Only a large safieh-print rug adorned the center of the room.

Emma drank the silence down into herself like an aromatic wine, aged and intensely intoxicating. Each time that she did, she relished it. She remembered the cacophony of music and laughter that was her daily rote as a child and accepted that now, what she loved even more than having her own space, was the quiet. Though It made her feel guilty, she couldn't bring herself to remember her childhood fondly. Instead, what she mostly recalled was a thankless existence full of messes and chores— a never-ending whirlwind of them—

and that every evening she was relegated to tidying as many things as her tiny hands could handle.

When she entered her kitchen, she was greeted by a tidal wave of sunlight. The kitchen was her favorite place to sit, with an unobscured view of her backyard if she looked down and a mesmerizing view of the sun rising over her busy neighborhood on the days she awakened early enough. But on this particular day, Emma walked into the kitchen, stopped short, and gasped the moment she crossed the threshold.

She ran back to the living room, grabbed her shoulder bag, and immediately began fishing for her phone again.

Emma's fingers were a blur across the screen as she looked for one number. *Here it is—Samuel's Landscaping.*

"Hey Ms. Pelly," Samuel dragged the long 'a' sound in his 'hey' when he answered, and Emma immediately took it as a partial admission of guilt for what she was sure his landscapers had done.

"Hey, Samuel," Emma took a deep breath before continuing. "I just came home and noticed that one of my kitchen windows is broken. It's the outer window; the inner pane is still intact, but the outer one looks like it'd shatter if I tapped it with my pinky."

"Well, Ms. Pelly, what exactly are you asking me?" Samuel's tone was tinged with apprehension. "Why are you calling me about it?"

"I'm calling you about it because—once again—there's a rock lodged between the inner and outer panes, and your guys cut my backyard this morning while I was out," Emma gulped hard, ready for the verbal battle that was to ensue. "So, what I'm sayin' is, one of their mowers dislodged a rock that shot straight through one of my windows...again."

Not today, Emma gritted her teeth. *He's not getting any sympathy from me today. Not one inch. Every time I do, he takes a mile. Why didn't I just fire him the first time? Why am I so full of second chances for every goddamn body?*

"I see," Samuel said slowly. "Well, I can't talk about it right now. Let me call my guys, and I'll call you right back."

He quickly ended the call before Emma could say another word. She let out a shaky sigh and looked at the time on her phone. She was ten minutes late for the meeting. Cursing under her breath, she dashed to the kitchen table, popped open her laptop, and signed into what she knew would be an uneventful virtual gathering.

This whole thing could've been an email, Emma thought after listening, halfheartedly, for nearly twenty minutes. She canceled her camera feed and was about to finish watering her plants as she listened to the rest of the meeting when a new email popped up in bold, flagged as urgent.

No.

Emma looked at the sender. It was Nathan again.

"No, no, and NO," Emma whined to herself, her finger hovering over her laptop mousepad.

She took a deep breath, clicked the email, and scanned it. "Really need a hand on this" and "you did such great work last time" almost brought a smile to her lips, but her tiredness withdrew it. She squinted at the rest of the email.

All of that bull and not a 'thank you' in sight, Emma read it one more time, hit reply, and started to type. Then, she stopped.

No, she thought as she closed the laptop. *Just...NO. I'm not gonna engage until I calm down first.*

Emma stood in her kitchen for a moment. She could hear the birds outside, and everything in her backyard looked lush and relaxing, even when she viewed it through the fractured glass.

I'm taking a break. Emma slipped on her sneakers and headed for the back door, then doubled back to get a bottle of wine and a package of snack crackers. *Nathan can manage on his own....at least for today.*

Emma sat on her back porch for a while, upturning her bottle of Chardonnay every few minutes as she watched the happenings around her. A squirrel sprinted across her privacy fence and leapt onto an overhanging tree. A wayward kitten mewed from somewhere close, but she couldn't pinpoint its location from the sound. Dogs barked energetically in response, and the mewing stopped. The succulent she'd placed in her terrarium had doubled in size, so she made a mental note to buy a bigger one to house it. She munched her crackers and turned her phone face-down on the glass patio table, enjoying the shade of her back porch. After some time, she ventured a few steps into the backyard and looked at her shattered window from the outside. The cracks in the glass formed an intricate spider web that refracted the light. Emma sighed.

Rocks, Emma frowned. *Why are there rocks back here anyway? Maybe left over from the foundation of the fence?*

She paced the lawn but found few rocks aside from smatterings of pebbles left over from the small areas of concrete poured for the fence. Determined, she circled back, looked down more carefully, and saw a pile of black rocks near the hedges closest to her back porch.

One of you is definitely the culprit. Emma saw that the size and shape of the rocks were similar to the one lodged in the frame of her now shattered window. She crouched and picked one up, nearly stepping on her braids in the process. *I've had a bit too much wine to be out here in the sun.*

She pocketed the stone and headed back inside. There, she dialed Samuel again.

"When can you have it replaced?" Emma asked after he answered with an annoyed sigh.

"Look," Samuel's tone softened. "I know you covered the damages last time, but I also gave you a few free services to even it out. Can't we work out something like that again? I mean, I thank God, you covered it the—"

"I do too," Emma said quietly.

"Excuse me?" Samuel sounded to Emma as if he was frowning through the phone.

"I do too," Emma continued. "I actually do 'thank God.' And I 'thank' the clerks in the store. I 'thank' people who let me over in traffic (on the rare occasion that it happens). I 'thank' my coworkers and my boss, and everybody else every day. I even thanked you for those half-ass services you gave me—which didn't amount to what I paid to fix that last window at all. So, when exactly am I going to get a 'thank you' for doing the right thing here? Since really, covering these incidents is part of your damn job?!"

"Alright, alright," Gerald swore under his breath and let out a warbly exhale. "Just calm down. I'll figure something out and get back to you. I still think it's strange, though. The same window in a year? This has never happened to my guys before. Anyway, I'll call you back."

He hung up the phone, and Emma felt gratified but slightly regretful.

It does seem strange, Emma chewed the inside of her cheek. *Yet, there's the shattered window clear as day, and he's the only one who had access. Guess I'll see how it goes.*

Emma nestled herself into her usual spot at the kitchen table and began to plow through her task list. After nearly two hours, she stood and stretched. As she walked to her coffeemaker to get a fresh cup, she felt something shift in her pocket and reached for it. It felt jagged and rough against her fingers. She removed the object and held it up in the light.

The bright colors in the dark rock shimmered as she rolled it in her fingers.

What kind of rock are you? Emma squinted at it, fascinated.

Abandoning her coffee errand, she slid back into her seat in front of her laptop and looked up the characteristics of the stone.

"Oh," Emma mumbled to herself. "You're really a crystal—carborundum."

In a few short minutes, Emma matched the stone by its picture and then researched it further. Her eyes scanned information about its origin, properties, and uses. In the end, she was only baffled by one aspect of it. She turned it over in her hand again, watching it curiously as its colors caught glints of sunlight.

Carborundum, huh? Emma mused. *How did you make your way to my backyard?*

Her phone vibrated loudly against the wood of her kitchen table. A text from Samuel.

"Hey, Emma. I think I've been more than fair, considering we're neighbors. I've let you pay late sometimes, and I cut the front and back yard for a reasonable price. With that said, I'm not willing to cover the cost of the window. If this means I'll be seeing you in court, so be it."

Emma stared at the text for a while. Her hands shook with rage. She typed several replies and erased them all before deciding on a simple one.

"Fine."

After she sent the text, she placed the phone on the table and walked to the island in her kitchen. She poured herself some more wine and stood there, calmly as she could, letting the bitterness of the liquid wash away some of her own. She heard the phone vibrate again but ignored it.

I guess it could be Anthony. Or maybe Samuel changed his mind.

It was Tanya. Emma rubbed the stone between her thumb and index finger in her right hand, soothed by its texture, and read the text.

"Hey, girl. Can I crash with you tonight? Lanae trippin' over some old shit, and I'm tired of hearing her mouth."

Emma flipped the stone between her fingers, then back into her palm. She read the text once more, then turned the phone face down on the table.

In no part of that raggedy text of hers did I get any form of 'thank you' for bailing her out this morning. Emma squeezed the stone tightly as she seethed. *Now, she's in another jam, and she wants my help? Nah.*

Emma ventured out to her backyard again. As soon as she opened the door to the back porch, the smell of rain hung in the air, dense as wet mud-cloth.

Emma balled her fists in frustration, and in the process, squeezed the stone so tightly in her hand that one of its jagged ridges broke the soft skin of her palm. *Shit! Is it too much to ask for a little appreciation from time to time?*

She dropped the stone near an overgrown tree stump in her backyard and stood examining the bloody scrape on the inside of her hand. The birds had stopped chirping, and the sky became dark. Thunder crackled in the distance. Emma looked at her shattered window once more and sauntered back into the house.

Hope it holds through the storm tonight without shattering. She looked at the sky, and as if in reply to her optimism, it darkened a bit more.

Emma went inside and tidied up the kitchen. She rechecked her phone. No response from Anthony, multiple texts from Tanya that she decidedly ignored. Finally, she turned it off and went into the small bedroom near the kitchen that she'd made into a home gym. Initially, Emma bought the home with the idea that she'd be settled with a need for extra space in a few years. After realizing it could be longer than that for it to become a nursery or an office, Emma eventually let it morph into a gym.

She went inside and spread out her yoga mat. As she flowed through her usual movements, she struggled to rid herself of the hassles of the day. By the time she was through, she had somewhat succeeded. She rolled up her yoga mat and looked at herself in the mirror.

At least that's one thing that went right today, Emma thought as she toweled off her forehead and walked toward the kitchen again. Halfway there, she heard a loud knock on the door.

She glanced at her watch. It was nearly seven.

What the hell is it now? Emma marched toward the door.

"Whatever it is, I'm not interested!" Emma called out as she approached it.

Then, she swung the door open without looking through her peephole and instantly regretted it.

"Hey, girl!" Tanya pushed past her with luggage in tow and tossed an overstuffed duffel onto Emma's couch before plopping down in the chair beside it. "Your phone off? I been calling you all day to let you know what time I was gon' be pullin' up."

"I was working, Tanya," Emma scowled at her seated friend. "You know, it's that thing I do to make the money I use to bail you out of your bullshit. Plus, I never agreed to let you crash."

"What?" Tanya sprang to her feet. "Well, where am I supposed to go? I don't have money for a hotel because I don't get paid until next Friday."

"Whatever, Tanya," Emma rolled her eyes and stormed off to the kitchen, yelling over her shoulder. "I want you out by 9 a.m. tomorrow, 'kay? I have a ton of work to do!"

"Damn," Tanya retorted. "I'll just camp out down here— no need to be so bitchy."

Forty-five minutes of hard-earned yoga Zen out the damn window in less than five minutes, thanks to her, Emma slammed her fridge door shut and chugged a glass of water before going upstairs.

Ascending the stairs, she caught snatches of Tanya's phone conversation.

"Yeah...looks like I'm stuck here for the night," Tanya sucked her teeth and continued. "I don't really know—maybe later. Nah. It's just us. She aint had a man over here in ages."

The sound of the boisterous laughter that followed burned in Emma's ears as she removed her makeup and dressed for bed.

Am I doing this right? Am I just here to be trampled on and used? Anthony is slipping away. Tanya is always around, but only because she needs something. Emma threw the used makeup wipe in the bathroom wastebasket and stared at the blackened, discarded wipe for a few moments before shutting off the light.

She crawled into bed and glanced at her phone. No

messages. She placed it on the charger stand and drifted away to the fuzzy sound of drizzle outside.

She dreamt of a throne and a gown with a train. There was a tiara atop her head. Flanked on both sides by beautiful, adoring servants, everyone curtseyed and bowed as she walked, and her long braids swayed behind her. Amidst the hushed conversations of her servants, another sound grew louder. Emma's eyes searched each corner of the decadent hall but could find no source for the noise, which sounded like a small animal mewing. Within moments it drowned out the other conversations and became deafening. Emma cupped her hands over her ears, but it was no use. The dream dissipated, and Emma sat straight up in her bed. Drowsily, her eyes found the outline of her phone on the nightstand, and she reached for it. It was 2 a.m. Then, she heard the sound again, just as loud as it had been in her dream.

What is that? Emma tiptoed down the stairs to follow the sound, which had become fainter. For a moment, Emma surmised that it must've come from outside and was about to turn back when she heard it again, muffled but close. As she stood at the landing at the bottom of her stairs, she took a moment to process what she saw in her living room before making a sound.

The television was on, with its volume low. Tanya was on

all fours, getting taken from behind. The man was muscular, his movements rhythmic and aggressive. His face was obscured by lengthy locs that reached his tattooed chest. Emma recognized her favorite throw pillow jammed into Tanya's mouth, and she suddenly felt something inside her tear at its seams. Once it came undone, she said her piece quietly.

"I need you both to leave," Emma said firmly.

Neither looked up from the act. The man had Tanya by the waist and was thrusting with such fervor that sweat glistened on his skin. Tanya clawed at the ground and writhed in pleasure, oblivious.

"I SAID I NEED YOU BOTH TO GET THE FUCK OUT NOW," Emma shrieked.

"Oh shit!" The voice was a baritone and had a calm tone, even though the man was clearly bewildered. "Aye, Tanya... I'm out."

In one impossibly smooth motion, he collected his clothes, keys, shoes and exited before either woman could utter another word. He closed the door softly behind him, and after Emma heard an engine roar to life outside, she faced Tanya once more.

"I have work in a few hours, but I'm not waiting until then," Emma said quietly. "Gather your things and give me some space, Tanya. You're out of fucking control."

"Ahh," Tanya said, nonplussed. "It's always about control

with you, isn't it? Sorry about the late-night company, but don't you think it's hella weird to barge in on us like that? You could've at least let me finish. Or maybe you just mad because you're not getting any right now."

"I am seeing someone—not that it's any of your business," Emma's voice sounded small to her own ears. "Why do you do shit like this to me? And how can you not see how fucked up this is?"

"Honestly, Emma?" Tanya's tone shifted from unbothered to aggrieved. "I just don't. I don't live a cookie-cutter life like you, and yeah, maybe that means it's not always predictable and stable, but at least it's not dry and boring. Like, what the fuck happened to you? And banging someone who barely spends the night or takes you out anymore hardly counts as 'seeing someone,' by the way. Emma...you do know that nigga's prolly married, right? I was gonna spare you that grim detail, but I swear, for all your book smarts, you're one stupid, uppity bitch sometimes."

The next few things happened too quickly for Emma to process that night. All she knew was that after a blur of tears, fists, hair pulling, swearing, and finally, a door slam, her friend was gone. Likely, for good.

Emma sat cross-legged on the floor after Tanya had gone, sobbing quietly with her face in her hands. Tanya's words rattled in her skull as she rocked back and forth, struggling to climb from under the weight of them.

Finally, she ran upstairs and snatched her phone from her bedside. She sat on the edge of her bed, pulled up Anthony's number, and called it.

It's nearly 4 a.m. If he's living with someone and they're quick enough, they are damn sure going to answer that phone. I hope they don't, though. I pray that it just rings and—

"Hello?" the woman's voice sounded hoarse. She cleared her throat and continued. "Who is this?"

Emma canceled the call and leaned forward, burying her face in her hands. She chucked the phone against her pillows and ignored it as it started to ring repeatedly. Tightening her robe, she abandoned the phone and went to the kitchen.

Guess I'm up now, Emma thought as she put a kettle on for tea.

Her head ached from the scuffle with Tanya, and her face felt puffy from hours of crying. She poured the hot water into her favorite mug and squirted a dollop of honey into the concoction before walking to her favorite spot in the kitchen. As she stood there, hands enveloped around her mug, she breathed in the smoke from the tea and closed her eyes. When she reopened them, she saw a dim light flickering in the corner of her yard.

Emma squinted at the pulsating light, eyes searching for a source. *What is that? Must be lightning bugs or something.*

Emma sipped her tea and let her mind wander. Restless, she paced the kitchen, tidying things out of place and thinking about the previous day's events over and over. Inwardly, she applauded herself for leaving her phone upstairs.

I probably would've still been on the phone with that woman up to this moment, arguing and shit...while his ass is sleeping like a baby," Emma scoffed and slurped the last of her tea.

She walked to the sink, deposited the mug, then turned off the lights. In an instant, everything was darker than before, except for the first light of dawn, slathering itself atop the night sky, orange and textured as marmalade. Then, another flicker, close to the ground.

It's coming from the same place—do lightning bugs stay in the same place? Emma tightened her robe and headed to the backyard in her slippers. She walked to the spot the light emanated from and crouched low. *Yup, Emma, you need to take your ass to bed NOW. You're clearly hallucinating.*

Emma crouched lower and examined what she saw: a mound of dirt the size of an anthill, surrounded by carborundum pebbles. On top of the mound, a tiny fire crackled. Among the pebbles were tiny people. Forgetting her robe, the dirt, and the thousands of hexapods that would usually have kept her from laying in her backyard without a blanket, Emma lay on her belly and stared at the miniature scene in awe.

And here I thought I'd seen everything there was to see back here, Emma mused. *I guess a hallucination from sleep deprivation doesn't exactly count, but hey, after the night I've had...I might as well just go with it.*

She propped herself up, dusted herself off, and jogged inside. She snatched her phone off her bed, sprinted out of the room, then turned on her heels and grabbed a quilted throw, too. Then she rummaged through a drawer until she found a phone stand. Back in the yard, sprawled on her belly, she propped the phone in its stand. She glanced at the slew of text alerts with Anthony's name on them and purposefully ignored them.

I'll deal with that crap later, she thought as she opened up the camera feature and zoomed in on the tiny fire.

Emma watched the little people and stones for hours. Every few minutes, she'd sit up, rub her eyes, close them for a few moments while taking a deep breath, then look again. Yet, each time, they were still there.

I... I need someone else to see this, Emma nodded to herself slowly. *Can't tell Tanya; I'm not even sure I'll ever speak to her again. It's too early on the west coast to call Natasha. So, I guess there's only one other person I know for sure who'd be into it. Ugh. Here goes.*

Emma hated to call Derwin but instinctively knew that he was the right person to call. She pulled up her contacts, then remembered that she never gave him her number for fear he'd overuse it. Of course, it was a rational fear. Emma thought back to how he'd like every picture she'd ever posted, showed up at every outing she and her girlfriends posted online in real-time, and sent her scores of messages on every social media platform he found her on. She knew from all her experience with him from high school to college, where they'd partnered in lab classes together that Derwin was a hard one to shake off. She also knew that the one thing they had in common was a shared love of science, sci-fi, and literature.

She messaged him and got an immediate reply.

Emma: Hey Derwin, what do you know about Carborundum?

Derwin: Tons. But who's asking? Does Emma know you're using her account?

Emma: It's me. Lol. I'm Emma.

Derwin: Prove it.

Emma hit the video call feature, and Derwin's eager face clicked into view. He was sitting in a dark room with anime posters plastered on every visible corner of the room. His desk was cluttered with soda cans, figurines, and books, and the glare from his laptop reflected as blue rectangles on the lenses of his thick glasses.

"Hey," Emma sat up and swept a stary braid behind her ear.

"Hey," Derwin stared at her, his mouth an "o" of

disbelief. "I—didn't expect your call, is all. Thought you got hacked."

"Nope," Emma shrugged. "Just been busy.

"Are...you outside on your lawn?" Derwin frowned, then chuckled nervously.

Emma smirked, then glanced down and saw the source of his nervousness. Her robe had slipped apart, nearly revealing her left nipple entirely. She snatched it shut and continued.

"I need you to look at something and tell me...just tell me what you see," Emma said firmly.

"Sure, I can do that," Derwin replied, his expression a mix of caution and subtle excitement.

Emma hit a button and flipped her phone camera's view toward the tiny fire. The scene looked the same, except that there were smaller mounds near the larger, initial one, and the fire was dwindling. Small figures made of leaves and dirt circumambulated the large mound in the middle. For several moments, neither of them said anything. Then, Derwin spoke.

"This is messed up, Emma. Really. Jeeeeee-sus," Derwin's tone darkened. "I gotta go."

"Wait—what'd I do?" Emma flipped the camera back to her face. "What's wrong?!"

"Is Tanya there too?" Derwin's thick brows cast shadows over his eyes as he continued, still scowling at her. "Is she filming this? I know I came at you a lot in college, and I get that you weren't into it; I made my peace with that. But now you call me out of the blue to prank me? Grow up, Emma. We're damn near thirty."

"I'm not up to anything, Derwin," Emma swept a hand through her braids. "I called you because I need you to tell me what you saw. I need to know that—I need to know that I'm not going crazy over here."

Emma wasn't sure if it was her lack of sleep or the emotional turmoil of the previous hours, but she told Derwin everything. She tearfully told him about Anthony's betrayal and Tanya's escapade on her living room floor. When she finished, he consoled her. When he was finished, she thanked him. Then, the tiny fire roared to life. But Emma didn't notice. She wiped her tear-streaked face and looked at Derwin with new eyes.

He's bigger than I remember, Emma's eyes darted from his dense mop of kinky hair to his broad, well-defined shoulders. His skin looks better too, and his teeth. Good for him.

"So, do you believe me?" Emma refocused her attention on her task. "Because I need you to believe me...and help me."

"I don't know, Emma," Derwin looked away, then leaned back in his chair and put his hands over his face for a moment. Finally, he continued. I need to see it in person. I'll bring some gear, take some photos. That's all I can promise."

"That's fine," Emma's shoulders sagged with relief. "I just

need you to help me make sense of it. I have so many questions."

Derwin acquiesced and took Emma's address and number. The moment she ended the call, she snapped back to reality.

Crap! I haven't even logged in yet—I probably missed a bunch of emails.

Emma jumped up and rushed back inside to her laptop and her work. For hours, her fingers were a blur across her keyboard. She cleared her task list distractedly, then looked at her phone after what seemed like an eternity.

He'll be here soon, Emma cussed under her breath as she rushed to shower and dress in time for Derwin's arrival.

She didn't bother with makeup. She didn't bother to sweep her hair up; they swayed gently behind her like a black, beaded curtain as she ran downstairs. She pulled on her sneakers just in time to hear her doorbell ring. When she opened the door, she saw that Derwin was standing on the porch with his back turned. He turned around at the sound of the door opening and gave Emma an apprehensive nod and sheepish smile before following her inside. He looked the same as he did on his video call, except that he wore no glasses. Emma could feel the nervous energy emanating from him and accepted it.

Shit, Emma frowned to herself as she led him to the

backyard. *He's probably being weird because he still thinks I'm crazy. Hopefully, that'll change in a sec. Or maybe I am. Guess we'll both know pretty soon.*

Emma had left her blanket and phone stand in the same spot. She took a seat and motioned for Derwin to do the same. When they were both seated, she propped her phone and zoomed in on the mounds again. Immediately, she saw that some things had changed.

"How is this—I mean...what is happening here?" Derwin's eyes widened, and his mouth hung open. "How are you doing this?"

"That's the thing," Emma stared at the phone screen, mesmerized. "I'm not."

The pebbles that were once scattered aimlessly around the dirt mound at their center had transformed into tiny structures. Obelisks and cubes, cylindrical and rectangular structures flanked the mound on all sides, and the creatures that once circled the mound without any obstruction now marched in single-file lines into each of the tiny structures before coming out the other end to access the mound. The mound itself was unchanged, except that the fire roared with a fiercer intensity than before.

"Oh my God—I've seen this before!" Derwin began gesturing frantically with his hands as he continued, and Emma shot him a sharp look when he almost upended the phone from its place on the stand. He chuckled nervously, dropped his hands, and continued. "This was a Simpson's episode. A Black Mirror one, too. Or Gulliver's Travels. It's a tiny society. Like, a mini-universe or something."

"Like the episode of Rick and Morty where there was a little universe inside their car battery?" Emma laughed incredulously. "There has to be some other explanation. Maybe they're just oddly shaped insects? Or maybe... I've got it! Come with me."

At that, Emma had Derwin check all the gauges in her home. They checked the knobs on her stove, checked the carbon monoxide detectors and the air filters. Then, they scoured the yard for mushrooms. They argued about what they'd seen in the backyard, checked the tap water in Emma's kitchens and bathrooms, then argued again. When they could come up with no logical answers, they checked the internet for articles about joint hallucinations. After reading as many as they could find, they ruled those out as possibilities too.

Once they'd finished with that, they took as many videos and photos of the tiny discovery as possible. They live-streamed it, posted about it, and spent the next hour fervently defending the authenticity of their posts. By the time they'd grown weary from that, it was dark, and the only light in Emma's backyard was that of the lampposts that lined her street and the headlights turning the corner adjacent to her home. Aside from that, there was still the persistent twinkle of the fire that burned atop the mound at the center of the minuscule carborundum structures and at the center of their attention.

"Nothing like arguing on the internet to wear you out, huh?" Derwin exhaled and slumped backward on his elbows with his knees tented slightly, his eyes affixed to the fire.

"Right," Emma let out a tired laugh. "If you lean back any further, you'll fall asleep out here, right under the stars."

"I would, but I'm actually hungry as hell," Derwin sat up abruptly, his brow creased at the sudden realization of his empty stomach.

As if in retort, Emma's stomach growled. "Yeah. Let's go inside. I need to check my emails, anyway. I haven't done a lick of work today, so I guess I'll be up tonight getting Nathan's stuff finished on time."

"Who's Nathan?" Derwin left the blanket and phone stand in place, as was their new protocol for their newfound excavation site and followed Emma into the house.

"He's this guy at work who does nothing, barely shows up, but always seems to be up for a promotion," Emma stood at the fridge, halfheartedly surveying its contents.

"I know the type...Chinese?" Derwin raised an eyebrow.

"What?" Emma frowned. "No, he's a white guy."

"No," Derwin threw his head back and laughed. "What I

meant was, should we order Chinese? You over there lookin' at the food in your fridge like they test questions or something."

It was Emma's turn to let out a hearty laugh. "I guess I am. I'm just so used to cooking for myself."

"I thought you were with that dude who's always on your social media," Derwin watched her intently. "Y'all aren't…together?"

"If you must know, stalker-person, that was never technically official, and as of yesterday, it's totally done," Emma said the words shakily, as if saying them aloud solidified them. She took a steadying breath and continued. "Yeah, he was lying to me the whole time, so it's basically over."

Shit! Shit! Shit! I don't want to see me in this weak-ass state. Come on, Emma. Suck it up. At least wait 'til he leaves before you have a meltdown.

"Hey," Derwin walked over and stopped a few steps short of Emma. "I didn't mean to trigger you. I didn't know."

"I know, but honestly, I'm just not in the right frame of mind tonight. Can we pick this up tomorrow? It'll be Friday, and we can work late." Emma could already feel the hot tears brimming her eyelids. She resisted them as hard as she could as she continued. "Tonight, I'm just too out of it."

"Oh yeah, totally," Derwin smiled sheepishly. "I'll grab something on the way home and check in with you tomorrow.

Get some rest, Emma."

Emma nodded, and as Derwin gathered his things, she watched him.

He's taller than I remember. And he looks better without his glasses. Really, aside from that same goofy smile, he's almost a different person now.

She walked him to the door and watched him get into his car and drive away before closing it. Then, she abandoned the idea of making dinner and climbed the stairs, her limbs heavy from the lack of sleep the night before. After her usual nighttime ritual, she reclined in bed and checked her messages.

Five emails from Nathan. None from Tanya—no surprise there. Emma jolted up in bed. *Fifteen from Anthony?! No, way. That could only mean…*

Emma read each text message from Anthony's girlfriend twice. Each one was lengthy, and once she was done, she felt the woman had told her an intimate story of her life without divulging her name until the end; Sharice.

Pretty name, Emma thought as she put the phone on her nightstand without answering any of the texts. *Sad story, though. Shit.*

Emma drifted off to sleep while trying to imagine the woman's face, and the face of the child she claimed to have with Anthony. She imagined them all in a perfect family portrait, smiling in front of a house with a two-car garage and picket fence in their matching cardigans. Then, her mind shifted to all the sex she'd had with Anthony in her home and in his car over the past few months, and the pleasantness of the dream faded. When the portrait of Anthony and Sharice resurfaced again in the dream, it was the same as it had been before, but their expressions had changed from jovial smiles to pained grimaces before the colors in the portrait began to melt away into the nothingness that surrounded it.

Emma woke up with a damp forehead and a thumping heart. The morning sun shone through her bedroom window in full force. She flopped backward and stared at the ceiling for a few minutes before dragging herself to the bathroom.

The rest of the day was a blur for Emma. She worked diligently for a few hours, sent Nathan an update on the project, then became distracted the moment she looked out her window. She checked her social media and saw that Derwin had sent requests for her to follow him back. She clicked "Accept" and scrolled through his posts and pictures.

Didn't expect so many anime memes and gym selfies, Emma mused as she browsed the photos. *His feed actually looks a lot like mine. Don't know if that's a good or bad thing, though.*

Emma's stomach growled, and her hunger snapped her away from her tasks, but she couldn't resist checking the backyard before she ate. When she approached the blanket and propped her phone in its usual spot, she gasped at what she saw.

"Can you get over here right now?" Emma gave Derwin a pleading look as he watched her from his end of their video chat.

"You're lucky my workday is almost over," Derwin smirked, then added, "and that you're cute when you're desperate."

"Whatever," Emma laughed. "Just bring food.

After he told her the time he'd be arriving, Emma went to the bathroom and adjusted her hair. Then, she added lip gloss and changed into a crop top and snug-fitting jeans. She looked at herself approvingly in the mirror when she was finished.

Wait—what the fuck am I doing? Emma frowned at herself in the mirror. *It's just Derwin, girl. Get it together.*

Emma looked at her phone. She had twenty minutes before Derwin would arrive.

Guess I'll go to my usual spot, Emma thought as she pulled on her sneakers. *That's all I have time for right now.*

She locked the door and paused, looking up and down the street, now bustling with school children celebrating the last days of a dwindling summer. Emma looked as far down the block as she could, sure that she saw a familiar car pulling away.

Couldn't have been him. Even his inconsiderate ass would've called first, Emma reasoned as she walked to her car. As she climbed in, a dark blue, late-model car screeched down the block and sped around the corner, nearly sideswiping her passenger-side mirror.

"Asshole!" Emma yelled after them.

But the car had sped away, and Emma couldn't make out the face of the person driving it, obscured from view by dark, tinted windows. Emma shook her head, pushed the ignition, and drove to the corner store.

Gerald beamed his toothy smile as soon as Emma entered. "Back for that wine?" he grinned.

"Actually...I guess I am," Emma replied sheepishly.

What am I doing? Is the wine for me and Derwin? Fuuuuck.

"Never mind," Emma frowned. "Just these."

She paid for her snacks and drinks and headed for the door. Halfway through it, she noticed that a man was trailing her. He was near the door but talking loudly into his cellphone. As he approached, Emma held the door for him. He pushed past her and continued to his car, continuing his boisterous conversation.

Are the words "thank you" extinct everywhere, or just here? Emma huffed inwardly and drove the short distance home, annoyed by the encounter.

Her phone began ringing as she walked up the stairs to her porch. She'd dug it out of her purse by the time she reached the door. It was Tanya.

Fuck does she want now? Emma looked at the phone vibrating in her palm and decided not to answer it.

"Want me to help you with those?" A familiar voice said behind her.

Emma turned to see that Derwin had parked and walked to the porch without her noticing.

"Sure, stalker," Emma laughed, surprised to find how easily her mood shifted at the sound of his voice. "How did you manage to sneak up on me like that? Just like in college. Creepy ass."

"Oh, that?" Derwin chuckled and pointed to his feet. "That's my trusty Vans. My best investment to this day. I can move like a ninja. Also," Derwin pointed to his small, silver car, "hybrids are pretty quiet."

Emma rolled her eyes and let Derwin hold her bags as she opened the door. A few minutes later, they made a small picnic with the spread of the takeout food and snacks on the blanket in the backyard and began their daily observations. The moment Derwin laid eyes on the site, he abandoned his meal and leaned in to capture some video.

"Whoa…" He stared, absorbed in the tiny scene in front of him.

"I know—it's crazy, right?" Emma said through a mouthful of lo mein. "But do you see the statue?"

"I do, but are you sure that it's—" Derwin squinted at the phone and zoomed in. "Never mind; that is definitely you."

"Right!" Emma continued excitedly. "So, I guess we're looking at a Lisa Simpson scenario? Maybe I'm being deified because I discovered them? And look how far they've advanced now. Insect chariots. Itty bitty light sources— probably solar, right? I mean, this is mind-blowing. I just wish there was a way to talk to them."

"Maybe there is," Derwin looked up. "If they're this advanced by now, then maybe they've learned to hijack our frequencies, Wi-Fi, etcetera. I think I can figure it out. It's silly, but I want to try something.

Derwin spent the next fifteen minutes scrutinizing the tiny structures, surveying what had transformed into a makeshift city with the statue of Emma at its center, until he pointed out what looked to Emma to be several indiscernible little hubs. Then, Derwin ran back into the house and produced his backpack, which he upended on the blanket, emptying it of its tools. Using several handheld gauges of different sorts, Derwin passed each one over the small patch of occupied ground and nodded expectantly with each beeping sound and read-out. Finally, he turned to Emma.

"I think they're building complex structures from the carborundum, and some of them are putting out a lot of juice for such a small area," Derwin paused for a moment, then continued. "I think it's safe to say that if we wanted to communicate with them, we could. But...should we?"

Emma answered without looking away from the statue at the center of the Lilliputian smattering of buildings and the odd figures weaving their way between them. "Yeah—I think I would." Then, she turned and looked at him quizzically. "So, what do you need from me? Extension cords? Batteries?"

Derwin put both hands on her shoulders and looked at her with both brows raised. "I need for you to relax, eat some of this food, and let me rig this up. I have a mini genny in my pack and everything I need to pick up whatever frequency they're putting out. At the rate they've advanced, I'm sure I'll have something compatible to work with."

Emma blushed at the feeling of his hands on her shoulders. Derwin's grip was firm but felt more reassuring than aggressive, and she found herself tongue-tied in the moment. She nodded at Derwin, and he dropped his hands from her shoulders and busied himself for the next hour. Emma watched him, popping grapes in her mouth as she worked at her laptop, catching up on all the work she'd missed.

Emma looked up to hear a crackling sound. It was Derwin, testing the knobs on one piece of equipment. He fiddled with it, turning it left and right. Then, they both heard it. It sounded at first like a low hum, then Derwin was at the knobs again, twisting them each carefully. Next, he pushed the volume on the device to its max, and they both gasped at what they heard.

"Yes, we are receiving," a warbled voice came through. "Ask of us what you wish."

"Ummm," Emma looked at Derwin, who shrugged. Then, she asked the first question that came to mind. "Why are you here?"

"We call ourselves Nemmians, and we are here because we were summoned," the warbly voice answered, and Emma noticed that a flurry of murmurs could be heard in the background.

"Summoned...how? And by who?" Emma leaned in closer, and Derwin did too, anxiously awaiting the answer with their faces so close that they could hear each other's breathing.

"You did, Braided One," the shrill yet authoritative voice answered after a brief pause. "You performed a blood ritual in a state of great anxiety, then set the sacred stones down in an ideal place near the Great Barrier and the Valley of Wood."

Great barrier? Emma's mind untangled each puzzling term slowly. *That must be the perimeter fence. And—and the valley of wood must mean the tree stump in the southeast corner, where I first found the stone. But what blood ritual are they—*

Derwin finished her thought aloud as if he'd authored the same one. "What blood ritual are they talking about? Did you do some kind of witchcraft back here? Because if you did, it would've been great if you mentioned that before."

Derwin asked the question in a playful tone, but Emma saw the apprehension in his eyes.

Think, Emma, think.

"I scraped my hand," Emma whispered, nodding slowly to herself. She looked up at Derwin and continued. "They must be referring to the day I found the rock lodged in my kitchen window. I brought it out here, and I was so upset that day that I was just like, gripping it tightly and walking around back here. Then, after that, I squeezed it too tight and cut my hand, so I just put it back where I found some similar-looking rocks. That has to be it."

"I guess you activated something that day," Derwin now stood with his hands on his hips. He looked down at Emma, still seated, then at the window. "I was gonna ask you about the window—what happened there?"

"It's a whole fiasco with the landscaping team that cuts my grass," Emma rolled her eyes. "This guy Samuel said he'd take care of it, then totally backed out. I was gonna take care of it, but then I got wrapped up in all this, I guess."

"Oh, okay," Derwin said, then added. "Well, you know my older brother does that kind of stuff—carpentry, windows, household repairs. I could ask him to look into it. One outer window is an easy fix."

"I couldn't ask you to do that," Emma could feel the heat

surging in her cheeks and was certain they'd turned a ruddy sienna by the time she continued. "It's no big deal."

"Well, technically, you didn't ask me; I offered," Derwin smiled. "And you're right, it isn't a big deal."

Derwin looked at Emma until she looked away, then went on. "We should record them, then compile this stuff and get it ready to push out to science journals, talk shows—whoever."

"You're right," Emma watched Derwin seat himself on the blanket next to her once more. "Let's get it done."

They spent the next two hours asking the Nemmians questions and recording the answers. Their first was about God, to which the communicator expressed a belief in, before adding that Nemmians had long ago cross-referenced their teachings against that of humans and decided that they all described the same divine source. That answer set off a domino of follow-up questions, which the Nemmian speaker graciously answered. When one of them would run out of questions, the other would take up the mantle with a fresh batch. After they'd learned the origin of the Nemmians and that the reason there were so many depictions of them in folklore was that they had always existed alongside mankind, they listened to the conditions of their arrival.

For this portion, Emma listened more intently, nodding to herself when Tinnik, the Nemmian who'd been speaking with them all night, explained that they only appeared when someone manifested them in a moment of great distress and with a blood sacrifice. They added that they could also be summoned on behalf of someone else, but that was more difficult. In each instance, if the one who beckoned them was successful, they would awaken slowly, congealing themselves from whatever was around them until they took on the form of the species that had summoned them.

Derwin listened with his mouth wide as Tinnik explained that there had been Nemmians made of candy wrappers, dung, leaves, paper, and soil, depending on the place they were called to "yield" themselves. After a long pause, Tinnik further explained that only certain sentient beings could summon them and that not all of those beings were human. Then, Tinnik continued detailing for Derwin and Emma their process for watching and listening to their subject, gathering all that they needed to build their odes to them; statues to express their gratitude and support. After other questions about the Nemmians' daily lives, Derwin asked the question that was most important to him, personally.

"Do you always use carborundum, and if so...how?" he leaned closer to the receiver, his head cocked to the side as he awaited the answer.

"There are many elements here that do many things," Tinnik's cryptic reply was coupled with a burst of laughter for the Nemmians around him, and Emma decided right then that it was one of the most pleasant sounds she'd ever heard.

"What do you mean?" Derwin pressed.

After a pause in which they both could hear a flurry of shrill murmurs from the Nemmians, Tinnik continued in a ceremonious tone. "A time ago that is now lost to most of your serious books and recollections, your kind was in tune with all the elements here. Those who had the loftiest knowledge could enchant the stones, plant them in the earth, and cities would spring forth. In time, the hatred between you brought war and separation, and some of those cities sank into the waters while others were abandoned.

"After many years, the numbers of those who could enchant the stones dwindled. We Nemmians still visited of our own accord, blooming where we were summoned, but mostly, we were forgotten too," Tinnik ended his explanation with a shaky sigh. "Yet, the fascination around the stones remains. Many wear them, study their characteristics, and place great faith in them. Unfortunately, the only stone that is harnessed for even a small bit of its power is carborundum. What if I told you that using the stone in your technology uses only an unfathomable small amount of its capabilities? But that is a conversation for another time. I am an elder here, and I am indeed tired from all this excitement."

"Of course," Emma nodded emphatically. "But...you said

you come to those in distress—so why did you choose me? I'm alright. I mean...I think...yes. I'm okay."

"Are you, Braided One?" Tinnik's voice lilted. "When we sprang forth, we sensed a great pain in you. We could smell it in the air—loneliness, loss, and sadness. Mostly, we sensed that you had no gratitude in your life, no thanks. It is why we erected a monument to you. It is a keepsake and ode. We've circled it many times, offering our Nemmian words to ensure a shift in your life. A shift toward your happiness."

"But I still don't understand, Tinnik," Emma felt the surge of tears but ignored them. "So, I guess what I'm asking you is, 'why me'?"

"It is because you are good, child," Tinnik finished, and Emma and Derwin could hear the cheerful murmurs of agreement in the background. "Goodnight, then."

The exchange ended abruptly, and the two sat on the blanket, their words suppressed by the weight of all they'd just learned. Finally, Derwin spoke.

"Emma, my bad for prying, but I just wanna say I had no idea you were going through so much shit," Derwin spoke and then looked away, first at the Nemmians' miniature city, then up at the sky.

"It's fine," Emma wiped her face, grateful that Derwin's eyes weren't on her as she did. "I'm not a total loser. I guess it's just that, on the day I cut my hand, everything was going wrong with my relationship, my best friend, my job—it was just a shitty day."

"No one said you were a loser, girl," Derwin landed a soft, playful punch on her shoulder. "Honestly. When Tinnik was telling you what he sensed in you, it felt like he was talking to me too."

"Derwin, your life is fine," Emma scoffed. "You've got a great job, you're smart as fuck, and you even managed to accept that you have to have that hairline shaped up if you want to be a valuable part of society."

"Soooo...what I'm hearing is that you sayin' I finally grew into my good looks," Derwin posed with one hand, stroking his beard, turning his head to different angles before breaking into a fit of laughter. "Seriously though, I feel like what I want is hella simple, and sometimes I get annoyed that it's always been so hard for me to lock down."

"And what's that?" Emma looked at Derwin, who had looked away again. Seeing this, she stared at what he was staring at, and there was a heavy pause between them as they watched the glittering lights in the diminutive Nemmian towers shut off one by one until only the lights near the statue of Emma's likeness remained.

"You know—a teammate, an intellectual equal, and…," Derwin glanced at Emma, who saw but pretended not to, then continued, "and a travel buddy."

"That sounds painfully simple," Emma smiled without looking up. "I think you have a pretty good chance of finding that. Ready to shut down for the night?"

Crickets chirped, and Emma could hear the scattered sounds of late summer swell to a zenith all around her. Cars zoomed by, and their bass-heavy music blared then faded, the aroma of charred meat wafted from the backyards, and dogs barked then held their silence in intervals too varied for Emma to predict. Right then, all the sounds and smells felt to Emma as if they were swirling around them both with powerful, centrifugal force, cocooning them in and prompting a moment. Ultimately, it was Derwin who answered it.

His eyes remained glued to the tiny city as he placed his hand on top of hers, but Emma could feel her breath stop short at her lips at the heat of it, the gentleness of it. For a millisecond, Emma remembered Anthony, but there was no guilt in the memory, only a brief comparison; there had been no intimacy between them. Not really. She knew that now. So, when Derwin finally looked up, Emma looked at him too and understood.

"Yeah," Derwin breathed words out, "let's go inside."

They left the equipment where it was and the blanket. They walked inside, hand-in-hand, and abandoned many things as they did. His touch having been enough, Derwin left all the words that caught in his throat each time he'd tried to express them in the past week. Words about how he was glad they'd become closer and about the way he'd always wanted it to be. Emma closed the back porch door on all the uncertainty she'd felt about Anthony, Derwin, and herself in the past weeks. For the next few hours, they barricaded themselves away from the world by consuming the safety and comfort of each other, uninterrupted. Those hours rolled into days together, then to weeks.

Eventually, after many late nights spent researching and cross-referencing the things the Nemmians had told them when they first established communication, Emma discovered that she and Derwin had slipped into a routine that was familiar to her in a way she didn't like. But each time she was about to probe Derwin with questions about outings and relationship titles, she found that she never got the chance. Before she could mount a complaint, Derwin was always at her door with tickets to art exhibits, dinner reservations, and ideas for other excursions.

Best of all for Emma was their mornings. She'd fling her arm to the other side of her bed and smile when her hands landed on the rising and falling of Derwin's bare chest. On those mornings, the room would be cloaked in sunlight, and Emma would revel in the moments before they rose to start their day because, in them, she had only a vague sense of the time. She was only certain today was Sunday and that Derwin was next to her, and she decided that both those things were enough for her. Out of habit, she tried to sit up and search for her phone, but Derwin's arms encircled her waist and pulled her close.

What is this? Emma's inner voice asked itself, dreamily. *Whatever it is, this is nice.*

She nestled herself against Derwin and remained until a loud knock stirred them both.

"It's probably a package or something," Emma groaned. "Sometimes they knock when they leave it. I'll check it out."

"You always tryna run from me," Derwin laughed with his eyes still closed. "Feels like college again."

Emma hit him with the pillow, and he recoiled in mock pain, still laughing. She paused before she left the room and looked over at him. His beige-brown body was entangled in her white sheets, and his chest was exposed from where she shifted the covers exiting the bed. She took in the broad nose, which suited his adult face more than it had when he was younger, and she admired how he'd grown his kinky hair out on top and cut the sides and back low, complimenting his square jawline. There was a tattoo on his left arm she hadn't noticed before, though: a woman. Emma squinted and made out the words "Cheryl" and two em-dashed numbers, which she instantly knew to be a birth and death date.

She pulled on a robe and headed downstairs to bring the

package in from the porch but swung the door open to find Anthony standing there instead.

I really need to start looking through the peephole every time, Emma sucked her teeth and readied herself for the confrontation. Because I'm sure, this is about to be some bullshit.

"You know," Anthony began. "When I read all that weird shit you and your goofy ass friend wrote on the internet, I just thought you'd lost it, so I gave you some time. Especially since I know my ex has been hittin' you up sayin' all types of wild shit."

"Okay…" Emma said calmly, wondering if Derwin could hear them.

"But now I see this nigga car out here day and night—and you aint hittin' me back," Anthony's tone shifted from angry to frenzied as he continued. "And I KNOW you fuckin' him."

"So?" Emma replied, even calmer than before.

"Fuck you mean, 'so'?" Anthony stepped closer to her, and Emma could smell the liquor on his breath.

"What I mean is, you never defined our relationship, barely returned my texts, and only pulled up to fuck," Emma could feel her hands shaking, and suddenly, a rage conjured itself from where it had been simmering in her gut and pulled itself out to rip and gnaw at the man who stood before her.

"You think I LIKED putting up with that shit? Huh? You honestly think that's what the fuck I deserved? Oh, and I know you fucked that petty bitch, Tanya. Heard about it at the hair shop, of all places. But hey, I guess that was better than me hearing it at a health clinic. FUCK YOU, Anthony. And your bitch. I blocked her weeks ago, anyway. Get the hell off my goddamn porch!"

Her stomach churned even now as she thought about it, but it was true. She had taken advantage of a day that Derwin had too much work to do to come over and decided to schedule herself a last-minute hair appointment. But, as soon as she walked into the salon that she'd long considered her self-care sanctuary, she overheard that Tanya had been in there the week prior, bragging about a revenge hook-up. Emma had sunk down in her chair, feeling sick as her hairdresser gleefully spewed the gossip to her, not knowing she was addressing the subject of it.

"Oh, that's how you REALLY feel, Emma?" Anthony took a step back, looked her up and down, and grimaced. "You know what? Yeah, I did smash Tanya. Been wanted to, actually. She thicker than you and she called me for the dick after you kicked her out your house like the moody bitch you are. Yeah. I know about that. She told me all about how you've been actin' stuck up ever since your other little friend left and I've felt that way too. You think you some bad, independent chick when you're really just a borin'-ass, workaholic bitch with no friends."

"Did she also tell you why I kicked her out?" Emma asked, smiling, her tone sweet. "The part about her getting back-shots on my living room floor? Took me half a day to get the smell out, by the way, and I didn't find a condom anywhere while I was cleaning up, so good luck with that. Did she also tell you that on that SAME day, I had to send her bum-ass forty dollars because she was stuck at another dude's house? I bet she didn't. Y'all are really full of shit. I tried to be good to her, just like I tried to be good to you. But now it's fuck BOTH of you."

Emma slammed the door in Anthony's face. Her heart pounded, and her hands still vibrated with rage. She stood on her toes, looked through the peephole, and watched Anthony storm off, nearly toppling two elderly onlookers out for a morning walk as he charged toward his car.

After he slammed the discolored door of his old sedan and pulled off, she turned away to walk back upstairs. Then, she heard the shriek of tires and ran back to the front window, parting the blinds in time to see the same blue car that nearly ran her over last time.

Who the hell is that? Emma shook her head and closed the blinds. *And what is their deal?*

The thought dissipated as quickly as it formed, pushed

aside by the dread that bloomed in her as she climbed the stairs to Derwin.

Did he hear us? Emma sighed. *If he did, he'll prolly just think my life has too much drama for him. But…I hope not.*

When she turned the corner at the top of the stairs, she could see that Derwin was sitting on the edge of the bed with his head bent and hands clasped. Emma approached anxiously, not knowing which reaction to expect, but when Derwin looked up, he gave her an apologetic look.

"I wanted to come down there and say something to him, but I wasn't sure if I should interfere—I'm sorry, Emma," Derwin reached for both her hands and pulled her onto his lap.

"Oh, that?" Emma looked at the floor. "I guess you heard everything, huh? My bad. I didn't know he'd pull up on me like that. Shit is embarrassing, to be honest. And you don't owe me anything. It's not like we're... you're fine."

"About that," Derwin scooted back and turned Emma around so that she was facing him, still in his lap. "I want those things I told you about that night. Do you remember? I—I still want all those things, Emma, and I want them with you…if it's cool."

Emma answered him with a kiss that turned into a late-morning lovemaking feat that left them spent and gazing up at the ceiling with their fingers interlocked. After a time in which they both said little, they made their way downstairs for breakfast. Halfway through their coffee, Derwin looked out onto the backyard and saw it. He tapped her on the shoulder, and then she saw it too. She dropped the coffee cup she was holding, and they both rushed to the backyard. From the porch, they could see that the padlock to the gate had been broken, and obscenities had been scrawled on each length of the wooden fence in red. Emma swallowed hard, let out a long shaky breath, and looked at Derwin, whose face bore the same dread as hers. Then, they both walked the short distance to their usual spot in silence.

The blanket had been balled up and thrown to the side. Derwin's audio equipment had been reduced to plastic shards. The tiny settlement, with all the gargantuan wisdom it contained, had been trampled to nothing. The intricate towers had been ground to particles, and the statue cracked in two. Emma's knees gave out from under her.

"I'll fucking kill him!" Derwin paced back and forth, swearing and covering his face with his hands in anguish. "This is some foul shit!"

Emma said nothing. Each word she tried to utter dissolved in her throat before it could form. She held the two pieces of the statue in her hands, hearing Tinnik's voice in her head. After a long pause in which Derwin observed her quietly, kneeling beside her and stroking her back, she rose and spoke.

"Well," Emma said. "It's not like anyone believed us

online. So, it's not that big of a loss, right?"

"Emma…" was all Derwin said, but Emma saw that his pleading was in the way he looked at her, and she heard it in his tone.

"It's fine," Emma brushed off her robe, turned on her heels, and walked inside with the tiny, broken replica of herself curled into her palm.

Emma listened to Derwin call the police. Then, she listened to the officer ask his questions about enemies, recent arguments, and many other things that soon became a blur in her mind. She listened to them urge her to file a restraining order against Anthony, which she agreed to and listened again as they consoled her and promised to call with updates. All of it, for Emma, sounded like words being broadcast underwater. She felt foggy and disconnected through it all and remained that way.

Derwin emailed her boss to inform her of the vandalism, then called the cousin he'd mentioned before to come to replace the window and power wash the fence. All of this he did while Emma stayed in her robe for days, in a stupor. Her braids became unkempt and dandruffy, and she drew the blinds closed in her room. Deep brown crescent moons darkened the underside of her puffy eyes, and Emma began to register just how much her work had meant to her. She sat the broken pieces of her Nemmian ode atop her nightstand and left it there amongst the wads of used tissues and empty glasses, until one day, she noticed that it was gone.

She sprang from the bed and searched again, then searched under the bed and on the dresser too. As she did, she caught a glimpse of herself.

You look like shit, Emma, she sighed and swept her hair up. *Wash your ass first, then look for it.*

By the time Emma emerged from the shower, she could smell something savory cooking. She dressed, put on some makeup, and pulled on a sleek black dress. On her way downstairs, she stopped, turned back, and put on a pair of earrings too.

He's been really patient with you, Emma looked at herself once more and headed downstairs. *Remember that.*

The moment Emma's feet reached the landing at the bottom of the stairs, and she looked around, she knew that she'd found her home in Derwin. She surveyed her plants and found that they were well watered, then peeked into the living room and saw that it was in perfect order. Overwhelmed, tears swelled in the eyes, and she put a shaky hand over her lips.

He took care of everything, Emma walked quietly toward the kitchen. *He took care of me without me asking.*

"Hey, there," Derwin smiled broadly as he stood stirring something in a large pan at the stove. "Look who's up and not looking like a zombie for the first time in days."

"Sorry about that," Emma sniffled and carefully wiped her eyes so that she didn't ruin her eyeliner. "I just felt like crap. I've never had a day like that day in my life. It totally threw me off course."

He put his hands on her shoulders, looked her in the face, and hugged her close in response. In his embrace, Emma felt herself become energized again. The horrors of the last few days dissipated as Derwin poured wine and piled her plate high. They ate their fill, and Derwin explained what he'd been up to during her rest. By the time they'd finished, Emma had learned several things, each more pleasing than the last. The first was that Derwin had recorded most of their conversations on his phone, and they had been saved successfully. The second was that he'd finally found a party interested in their work—a publisher interested in a didactic compilation of their findings, images, and audio.

"They did say that we'd have to publish it as fiction, though—does that matter?" Derwin raised an eyebrow.

"Nope," Emma smiled and leaned back in her chair, satiated. "I don't mind at all. What's the other news?"

"This," Derwin reached into his pocket and produced the fully restored Nemmian miniature. "For you, 'Oh Braided One.'"

Emma stared at it in awe. Her lip quivered as she held it. "Thank you, Derwin."

"Actually, I should thank you," He leaned forward with his elbows on the table and covered her hands with his before continuing. "Even though it ended in a messed-up way, you brought me along for this. I'll admit that it's not how I envisioned I'd reconnect with you, but honestly, I wouldn't have cared what brought me back; I'm just really glad to be here. And I know I've been spending a lot of time here, and been going back and forth to my place, but I want that to change. I want us to do this book thing together. I want us to build something together and maybe get a fresh start somewhere new...if you'll have me."

Emma let the warmth of his gratitude ease her, like the balm that it was. She sat back and looked at the newly replaced window and the cleaned fence. She looked at their empty plates and then back at Derwin and felt her connection to Derwin deepen. She nodded, unable to speak, but Derwin understood.

It took them eight months to draft the work the publisher requested, then a few more to edit and launch. In a few short weeks after its release, The New Nemmians was an acclaimed hit, and Derwin and Emma were back at her kitchen table, scanning through their share of the profits and planning their future. A few months after that, they packed up each of their homes and relocated to Northern Virginia. After two exhausting weeks of unpacking and decorating, they stood in their new kitchen, which looked out onto a new backyard.

"We forgot to get paper towels," Emma called to Derwin, who was seated at his desk in the study. She waddled over to the French doors and peeked in, one hand on her swollen belly. "Want me to go pick some up from the corner store?"

"Sorry to break it to you, my little ghetto queen, but there are zero corner stores around here," Derwin laughed heartily. "You mean the 7-11? We might as well go to the grocery store, girl. Gotta start shopping like we're a real family at some point."

"Guess you're right," Emma giggled.

Leaving the store, Emma was about to climb into the passenger side of Derwin's SUV when she spotted a blue car. She paused and stared at it for a moment.

That car. It looks like...but it couldn't be, could it? Emma's face crumpled as she struggled to remember. *Still, wouldn't hurt to see who gets into it, though.*

After a few moments, a woman walked toward the car with a toddler in tow. She was a tall, frumpy, macadamia-colored woman with reddish hair pulled back tightly. Her face looked haggard, and there were small stains on the baggy tee she wore. She held the small child's hand in her right and carried groceries in her left. She also carried an oversized shoulder bag that looked more like luggage than a purse to Emma. As she approached the car, her phone rang, and she dug in the pocket of her dingy sweats to retrieve it.

"Hello...this is she...this is Sharice," the woman cradled the phone between her ear and shoulder as she loaded the child, then groceries into the blue car. "I can't today. Why? Because I covered for her yesterday, that's why."

Upon hearing the name, Emma froze, and an unfinished piece of the puzzle that she and Derwin had struggled to complete finally fit into place.

Sharice, Emma's eyes remained glued on the woman, who was still preoccupied with what sounded like an annoying work call. *As in, Anthony's Sharice.*

Emma continued to listen as close as she could, but Sharice ended the call. Moments later, the engine roared to life and the car's rear headlights flicked on as Sharice prepared to back out. Then, the car stopped and Sharice emerged again, cursing and scanning the ground. Emma watched her pick up a small toy, wipe it off, and hand it through the back window to a small pair of waiting hands. Then, her talon-like nails became a blur against the phone's surface, and she began to yell at the person on the other end. Emma listened as words like "deadbeat" and "tired" and "help" cut the fall evening air and caused onlookers to scurry by the angry scene. Finally, she returned to car, backed it out of the spot, and drove toward the exit of the grocery store parking lot. For a millisecond, Emma saw her face clearly as she passed, and she could see that her face was drawn and haggard. She could also see that she was in tears.

Emma stared out of the window for the duration of the short ride home. She looked down at her engagement ring, then over at Derwin. When she looked out again, she saw that the sun was sinking fast, and they were nearly home.

The next morning was a Saturday, and Derwin left for the gym, offering his customary dad-bod joke on his way out the door. When the sound of his engine faded, Emma settled into his desk chair with a bowl of grapes and a singular task. She pulled up every one of Anthony's social media pages and navigated to each one until she found one that she wasn't blocked from. From there, she searched through his long list of followers, rolling her eyes at the scores of half-naked women before she saw the familiar face. She opened the page and gleaned as much information as she could from it. Then, she pulled out her credit card and purchased a dossier on Sharice. The whole endeavor took an hour, and twenty minutes after she had finished, she was parked several doors down from the home of Sharice T. Moore.

Emma wore baggy, dark clothes and large sunglasses and walked as casually as she could. As she approached Sharice's front yard, she could see that the mailbox on the porch was overflowing with mail, and some of the envelopes were red. Worn looking toys were scattered on the yard, and its perimeter was overgrown with weeds. Emma looked left and right, swung the door of the chain link fence inward, and walked inside. She peeked through the gaps in the shabby blinds that cloaked the inside of each window but could make out very little.

I need to do this quickly, Emma took a deep breath, hoping that she had given her pain meds enough time to kick in. *I need to do it now and get out of here...because I'm not even sure it's going to work.*

Emma chose a small bush on the side of the house and crouched low. She reached into her jacket pocket and pulled out a large piece of carborundum and a paring knife. She whipped her head left and right again to see if anyone was approaching, then dug into her left hand with the paring knife, drawing blood. Pain bloomed from her palm as a steady, pulsating thud, but it was faint. She wrapped her bloody fist around the carborundum and squeezed with all her might.

Tinnik? It's me, Emma, she closed her eyes and focused on the request as hard as she could. *Nemmians, if you can hear me, or sense me, I need you to fix this. I know I should hate her—and maybe you should too—but I don't. I think... she's been broken. But far worse than I ever was. So, I guess...if you can hear me, help her. Thank you.*

Emma placed the stone down and pressed it into the earth, projecting all the healing she wished for Sharice into it. As she did, she realized right then, crouched low near her would-be enemy's porch, that she had changed. Through an odd series of events, Emma had learned to weave closure, forgiveness, and gratitude into her life. She put a hand on her belly and realized that those three things were what she needed for the next chapter of her life, and they overlapped each other with a rhythm that moved mountains and altered the universe.

Emma promised the life budding inside her that she would braid those three things into their existence every day. She vowed to be like the Nemmians in that way. No matter where she planted herself, and no matter where or how she bloomed, she would never forget.

Chimera Agent

Dinah could feel a pain swelling behind her temples. Her mouth felt dry and sticky. She checked the waiting room again.

Two more, she sighed. *Good.*

She sat down at her desk in the intake area and finished up the last of her paperwork, glancing at the clock periodically.

She's late again and if she doesn't get in here in five minutes, there'll be no one here to relieve me. Then, I'll end up stuck here for another half-hour doing intake for the next two, Dinah thought as she stood up and headed for the door.

"Gone already?" Daniel said nervously over his shoulder from the front desk.

He smiled feebly, but Dinah recognized the same weariness in his eyes as he spoke. His short-sleeved shirt he wore that day revealed his tattooed forearms, and Dinah spied the slopes and lines of a familiar one on his inner wrist. She had the same one on her wrist but chose to cover it in public. When Dinah met Daniel for the first time, it was how they verified each other. Their markings, and the amethyst irises of their eyes.

"No," Dinah returned the half-hearted smile, as was their ritual. "Just the restroom. Let Margaret know where I'm at if she decides to show up."

She could hear Daniel chortle as she sauntered toward the restroom.

The motion lights in the bathroom flickered on lazily, and Dinah staggered to the sink and leaned on it. She turned the water on, put her left hand under it, and hissed.

Dinah watched as the redness from the chemical burn on her left hand healed itself. "How can they drink this?"

Dinah's throat tightened from thirst at the mere thought of water. She reached in the left pocket of her scrubs for her tin of capsules, rummaging frantically, then searched her back pocket. Finally, she pulled both of her cardigan pockets inside out, but produced only worn tissues and a packet of gum.

She glanced in the mirror again to see that her true, bluish tint was beginning to show beneath the tawny, golden undertones of her skin, and the effect was that she began to look greenish under the fluorescent lights. Even the coils of her hair, which she'd swept up and secured into a neat updo that morning, had already begun to look withered and dry.

I can't wait 'til we're done with this project, Dinah gripped both sides of the sink and stared at her face, which had begun the subtle flaking that it always did when she forgot to dose on time.

Dinah heard something hit the floor. The sound of it was dry, like a wood chip or dead leaf. She squinted at the checkered surface, then stooped down when she spotted the brown, dime-sized, crumbly lump on the floor that had, moments ago, been a portion of her left ear. Something sparkled in the midst of the mass—an earring.

My earring. Damn it—my ears can't even hold the weight of an earring when I'm withering and molting like this. Dinah undid her hair and carefully maneuvered it to cover her left ear until it healed.

She examined the lobe after she finished and saw that the missing area of flesh was already filling itself in, but the process was slower than usual. She sighed, washed her hands for as long as she could bear, then headed back to the intake station of the hospital emergency room. By the time she walked back, the chemical burns from the sink water had crusted over and begun to heal.

Dinah came back to her desk to find that Margaret was already settled in and working. She raised an eyebrow at the rare scene.

"So sorry about being a few minutes late," Margaret said as she gestured like a street magician, a trait Dinah quickly learned to look for when the young nurse was lying. "The parking lot was just so jammed, ya know? Anyway, I've already put the vitals in for the first one out there."

She's an energetic one today, Dinah mused, eyeing her lackadaisical coworker curiously. *That's a pleasant change.*

"It's no problem at all," Dinah smiled at her and felt a back tooth wobble. "But umm…did you happen to see if Allen was behind you? I know Daniel's supposed to be off right now too and I think he's supposed to be relieved by Allen today."

Margaret twirled the end of her ponytail on her fingertips, "No. Come to think of it, he rushed out a few minutes after I got here. Allen shouldn't be long though."

Dinah nodded in response and began surveying her desk with a scowl.

"I know this is random, but did you happen to see a red tin of mints near my workstation?" Dinah tried to sound less anxious as she continued. "Maybe Daniel took it?"

"Oh, this?" Margaret held up the tin and shook it until its contents rattled. "I was just about to ask if I could have one—"

"No!" Dinah screamed and snatched the tin, then saw that several heads in the waiting room had turned towards them. She lowered her voice as she continued. "I mean, those are pretty hard and stale. Just can't seem to throw them away…bad habit, I guess. I was just about to get a snack from the vending machine on my way out, though. Did you want anything?"

"Nah," Margaret replied, with a concerned look on her face. "It's time for you to punch out and I'd hate to hold you up. See you tomorrow, 'kay?"

"Cool," Dinah tried to hide her relief. "Bye, then."

Dinah grabbed her things and rushed to the elevator.

Late because of parking? Yeah right, Dinah scoffed inwardly as she exited the elevator into the deserted parking lot.

Dinah didn't let herself focus on Margaret's lie. Instead, she looked left and right to make sure that no one was watching, then ran full speed to her car. Once inside, she slammed the door, popped open the tin with shaky hands, and shook two capsules into her palm. She swallowed them and felt the capsules move slowly and painfully down her parched throat. Then, she looked at her reflection in the rearview mirror and watched as the fullness returned to her cheeks, and the color flushed back into her skin.

As she pulled into her driveway at home, she saw that her door was ajar. She quickly maneuvered backward and drove away, recalling the protocols Gideon had installed in her before she and Daniel began their work on the surface. Her heart thumped for the full eight minutes it took her to get to Daniel's place. She parked half a block from his split-level rancher but didn't see his car.

If he's not there…that means we've been compromised, Dinah chewed her bottom lip. *But how?*

Dinah's phone vibrated in her cup holder, and she jumped. She scooped it up and checked the number. It was unknown. Apprehensively, she accepted the call.

"Leave everything, Dinah," a familiar voice said on the phone. "I got word from Daniel that Margaret took one of your capsules. He told me that he tried to stop her, but she'd already grabbed them off your desk before he could reach her. He left work in a hurry after that. Spoke to him about an hour ago. But really, Dinah? Your desk?" Gideon sighed into the phone. I know the Chimera Program is a long-haul project, but it's a crucial mission, nonetheless. You heard the elders—if this doesn't work, we'll have to pull out the big guns, remember? Anyway, you were pretty careless today, so now you'll have to move."

"What?!" Dinah slammed her hand against the steering wheel. "She told me she didn't touch them!"

"It doesn't matter, Dinah," Gideon continued. "I warned you that your whole 'I'll hide them in plain sight' idea was a bad one. Anyway, I'm sending you the coordinates of a safe house. I've decided to keep you and Daniel separated for a while so that if the worst happens, at least one of you will be safe. In the meantime, I'll scout a safe place for you both to submerge. I need about 18 hours, though. If you don't hear from me before then, just head back to Daniel's and I'll intercept you there."

"Got it," Dinah killed the call and drove to Baltimore in silence. She paid the fee for the temporary lot and found a spot far from the entrance with larger vehicles on each side.

After she parked between a pickup truck and passenger van, she checked her wallet, capsule stash, and glove compartment. Under a pile of car documents, scented tree air fresheners, and a canister of moist towelettes, she found the screwdriver she was looking for and tucked it against the small of her back. Then she popped the trunk, slid in the backseat, and opened the rear passenger door to avoid being spotted near the front of the car.

She looked around, then popped the trunk and retrieved the emergency backpack she'd stashed inside after Gideon had given her the car. She unzipped it, pocketed a handful of forged documents and some cash, then she pulled on a lightweight hoodie. She pulled the hood over her hair, crouched low, and started on the plates to her car. As she unscrewed them, she willed herself not to cry or sweat.

Can't waste my body's water, Dinah reasoned as she put the plates in the backpack. Then, she climbed into the backseat, locked the doors, and laid there with her knees tented uncomfortably in the cramped space. She stared at the ceiling of the car until she felt drowsy, then set an alarm on her watch right before drifting off to sleep.

***

The next morning, as soon as she saw the first hint of sunrise, she abandoned her car and former life along with it.

Dinah walked for hours, missing the powerful air conditioning of her abandoned car all the while.

She kept her head down for the first two hours, then reluctantly shed her hoodie during the third. The slight trickle of pain that sprang from her temples was now a raging waterfall with a forceful current, throbbing behind her eyes. She sat down at a bus stop to rest. The man sitting next to her was noisily chugging a plastic bottle of water.

Must be nice to be able to drink that and live...or maybe not, Dinah's thoughts raced as she massaged her temples. *But as for me...I need real water; I need a capsule.*

She pulled her backpack to her lap and unzipped it, clawing through the clothes, toiletries, and folded documents for the capsule tin. Nothing. Then she unzipped the front pocket and dug in. Her fingers felt along the rolled-up socks and underwear, then finally brushed against the coolness of the tin.

Finally, Dinah pulled the tin out and was about to pop it open when she overheard a newscaster's voice.

"I'd like to welcome Margaret Turley to the show today (audience applause). So, Margaret, tell us more about this miracle capsule you've been taking? It's all over social media and people are ready to get their

hands on it…"

Overhearing the broadcast, Dinah tucked her tin back in her backpack and slung it over her shoulders again. She could feel the tiredness in her bones now—the degeneration that washed over her each time she went too long between doses. She forced one foot in front of the other and began to pick up speed until she was trotting.

When she spotted a drug store, she ducked in and bought a baseball cap and some sunglasses. Then, in an alley next to the store, she looked left and right, whipped out the tin again, and opened it. As she pried it open, her thumb nail peeled away and fell to the ground, crumbling on impact. Dinah downed the capsule and gently touched her left side. The slits along her flanks, which served as gills each time she swam, felt sore and oozed a clear liquid. The sweat and friction from her run had irritated the openings so that they propped open slightly, revealing pink flesh that resembled the bellows of an accordion. She downed another and watched them reseal until they were nearly undetectable again.

Good, Dinah lowered the left side of her shirt, pulled the baseball cap low and exited the alley as casually as she could. *I'm shedding too much water in this heat and I'm burning through my stash quicker than usual, but at least I'm almost there. Just fifteen minutes away.*

She passed several eateries as she walked down the thoroughfare. Couples dined outside and passersby moved merrily beneath the setting sun as they walked their dogs and ran errands. A woman with a small child walked briskly toward her car. As she loaded the whining girl into the car, Dinah saw that the girl had a sparkly bookbag with a mermaid on it slung over her shoulder. The bikini-clad figure on the pink bag had long, red tresses and was perched on a rock amidst sparkling turquoise waters, smiling and petting a dolphin.

They sure make us look glamorous, Dinah smirked at the woman, who turned around and shot a look at the creepy woman in glasses and a hat, staring at her and her child. *Whoops—guess this outfit is not exactly long-stare-friendly.*

Dinah pulled her brim down a little more, quickly crossed the street, and tried once more to blend in. She also tried not to appear as if she was listening too closely to anyone's conversations, but she couldn't help but catch snatches of it as she continued her trek to the safe house.

"You're right! She said it cleared her fibroids and vision, and her mother's cancer tumors are gone. She has proof from her doctor. He came on the show with her..."

"Allahu Alim. How should I know? Maybe the pill is like the zam zam water. You know? Like that so-called magical water from the Middle East? Either way, I set my phone alerts for updates because I

wanna know when those capsules go on sale…"

"I hope they track down the woman who gave them to her. They showed her picture during the show, but it was from some grainy work ID. Man, I'd love to ask her where she got those things. I've tried everything but I can't seem to find any info online about them. Maybe she brought them from another country?"

GAVE them to her?! Dinah was furious. *Margaret STOLE them from me then LIED to my face about it. Now there's a freaking manhunt for me and I have to go into deep hiding for months waiting for this melee to die down. I'll have to work in another goddamn hospital to scout candidates and stay there indefinitely. And if I fuck up again, Gideon is gonna kill me before these crust-dwellers do.*

Dinah pulled herself from her inner tirade and discovered that she'd arrived at the address. It was a sprawling cape cod with well-kept hedges around the perimeter of its large lawn. The door was slightly open, and she could hear voices inside. She took a deep breath, and walked in.

This isn't like the other stash houses, Dinah moved through the house cautiously, her eyes pouring over its details. *Looks like someone still lives here.*

The television was on in the living room. Dinah listened for a few moments and recognized that it was the same broadcast that the man at the bus stop had been listening to earlier. She saw that the furniture looked new, and the hardwood floors were spotless. Then, she entered the kitchen and noticed that there were three glasses in the sink, and that the back door was ajar. The voices she'd heard earlier had stopped, too. She stepped forward, then paused.

"Maybe the voices were just noise from the TV, but still—something's not right here," Dinah whispered under her breath. Then, louder, "Is...is anyone here?"

She closed her eyes and took a deep breath to steady her nerves. *Get it together, Dinah. Gideon vets these places all the time. It must be safe. It has to be.*

She pushed the back door, and it swung it open with a creak. Slowly, she stepped out onto the back porch. Her hands shook uncontrollably, but she took another nervous step forward and looked around.

Everything looks normal enough, Dinah thought as she moved toward the back porch stairs. She closed her eyes and sniffed, searching for her guardian's scent in the air. *Good. Gideon's here. In fact, he's close.*

She took another step forward and nearly tripped on something solid in her path. It was covered in a heavy tarp, but Dinah could see a pair of feet protruding. She knelt and pulled the tarp back,

Gideon! Dinah put her face in her hands and sobbed.

Before she could wipe her tears and stand, something struck her in the back of the head, and darkness enveloped her.

Dinah awakened to something cool touching her skin,

and quickly realized it was a metal table. She squinted at her surroundings under the harsh fluorescent lights.

These lights are...too bright, Dinah tried to lick her lips, but found she had no saliva. *I'm being wheeled somewhere...but where?*

She strained to remember the last thing that happened, but the throbbing pain at the base of her neck blotted out all memory. She reached to massage her temples but discovered that she couldn't; her arms were fastened to a gurney in an immovable way. She heard voices around her, but none she recognized.

"Hey!" Dinah tried to voice her protest, but her voice called out in a cracked whisper that was barely audible. "What is this?! Where are you taking me?"

The uniformed men wore helmets, said nothing, and ignored Dinah altogether. Then, she heard a series of metallic clicking sounds and realized that the person who had been wheeling her forward had stopped and was now propping her upright and angling her forward. Slowly, the sights and sounds around her coagulated into one picture and the person in front of her came into focus.

"Miss Clark—Dinah Clark?" The woman's tone let Dinah know that it was a question. "We don't have much time here, seeing as though your colleague didn't last very long, so I'm going to ask you this nicely—one time—before I move on to other methods of interrogation."

"What?" Dinah asked, though she wasn't sure at that moment what her 'what' was for. She paused, then shifted her focus to a different word.

"Where...where are we?"

"That's not important," the woman snapped.

She was a petite, shrewd looking woman. Her hair was pulled back tightly, and her small, piercing eyes shrank into her face as she glared. When she started to speak again, Dinah saw that her left eye twitched slightly as she did.

"What I need from you is simple," she continued. "Just tell me where you got the capsules and there won't be a need for any unpleasantness. Do you manufacture them?"

"No," Dinah answered, her mental fog finally dissipating.

I'm in a facility of some sort, but these aren't medical personnel at all, Dinah shut her eyes and tried to rationalize. *These look like the military type, but the uniforms look different. No name tags. No ranks. Whatever this is, it isn't right. This is exactly what Gideon warned me about.*

Just as quickly as her thoughts began to coalesce, a lightning-fast blow landed against her cheek. Dinah struggled against the restraints, but it was no use. She felt blood trickle from the corner of her mouth.

"I asked you a question," the ponytailed woman began, then switched to a sweeter tone as she continued to probe. "Apologies, where are my manners? I'm Dr. Sophia Bartelli and you'll find that I prize efficiency over all else. This means that, if I ask you a question, I expect an answer, Dinah. Clear?"

Dinah nodded woozily, then sputtered, "I don't make them. I-I can't. That's not how it works."

"Then what is it?" Dr. Bartelli began pacing as she continued, and Dinah was relieved.

Maybe she won't hit me as much if she keeps moving like that, Dinah tried to put a hand to her swollen cheek, but then remembered she was restrained.

"A bioweapon?" she continued.

"No, nothing like that," Dinah said calmly.

"An enhanced street drug?" Dr. Bartelli continued pacing. "Is that what it is? How are they able to mask its properties? I've had countless people look at it and as far as we all can tell, it's nothing but—"

"Water," Dinah finished.

Dr. Bartelli stopped abruptly. "What do you mean?"

Dinah laughed, and the guards shifted uneasily. Hearing the collective sound of them moving their hands to their weapons and adjusting their stances, Dr. Bartelli raised a hand to quiet them, patting the air in a gesture that told them to calm down.

"I mean exactly what I said, actually," Dinah spat blood on the ground and wiggled a back molar with her tongue before continuing. "It's pure water. That's it."

"How was it purified?" Dr. Bartelli's eyes were wide. "Through what process? Or is it glacier water? No... that doesn't do what this can do. Patient zero is in bad shape, but for days before that, she was in—as she and the doctors put it—the best shape of her life. She was ill before then, though, and that makes it hard for us to quantify if the capsules failed her because of her preexisting condition. What we need are efficacy trials on controlled subjects, and we need them now. So, you see, we just need to know what's really in them."

Dinah laughed again, and her loose tooth throbbed harmoniously with the pain searing through her cheek.

I thought that maybe her slap loosened it, Dinah pored over her dwindling options. *But it's not that at all. I'm out of capsules. They were in my pack, and I have no idea where that is now. Guess this means I'm finally out of time.*

"Look, Dr. Bartelli," Dinah hung her head. "Capsules won't help you. I'm guessing my old coworker, Margaret, was patient zero, right?"

"Correct," Dr. Bartelli stood eerily still, and Dinah wasn't sure if she had truly calmed down or was readying herself to pounce again.

"And she's dead now, correct?" Dinah pushed the words out in a measured tone while keeping her head down and wheezing softly between words.

This dehydration is crippling me, she let the realization wash over her as she looked up to find Dr. Bartelli nodding "yes" in answer to her question.

"The public doesn't know that…and nether should you," Dr. Bartelli pursed her lips and continued. "But yes, she's deceased."

"Well," Dinah could barely manage more than a whisper. "What's happened to her is similar to what's happening to me right now, but in reverse."

"In clear terms, Ms. Clark," Dr. Bartelli's voice was laced with frustration.

"She died because everything about the water I drink isn't safe for her in large quantities, and I'm dying because the water that she consumes every day is poison to me and others like me. It's poison to everyone on the surface, really. You're all just better acclimated to it.

"I'm from a place where there is pure water—purer than the lakes, oceans, seas, and springs your kind has decimated, and cleaner than the water in the polar ice caps you've managed to diminish so rapidly. Unfortunately for you, your bodies can no longer process pure water properly. Most of you would perish during the intense therapy required to reverse the damage your water has done to your bodies. So, about 100 years ago, my people installed chimera agents—surface dwellers imbued with some of our physiology and thus able to withstand your water, and ours. Our goal was to intermingle and produce offspring that could survive the next hundred years on the surface without the aid of our capsules, but we haven't been able to quickly enough. And that's partially because, at the rate in which you're poisoning your water, neither of our kind stands a chance."

Before she could continue, Dr. Bartelli turned and walked through a set of double doors, yelling over her shoulder as she went.

"Bring her," she said as her short heels clicked loudly toward her destination. "Let's keep her alive for now."

In seconds, Dinah was flat on her back again. Her straps were readjusted, and she was being wheeled forward. She shut her eyes tight and listened to the crunch of the guards' rubber-soled boots keeping time with the squeak of the gurney's wheels.

She was wheeled into a room much dimmer than the hallways and propped upright again. Then, two of the guards undid her restraints. Dr. Bartelli nodded at the guards, who grabbed Dinah by the elbows and led her to a chair at the room's center. The room was lined with a few monitor stations, and Dinah observed that there were drain grates in several areas of the linoleum floors, and a surgical table near the chair.

Well, Dinah gnawed her dry bottom lip, frustrated. *This looks more like a kill-floor than a lab or medical facility, but whatever she wants to do, she can do it. Nowhere to swim from this. No Gideon to call.*

She sat down in the chair with a thud and stared at Dr. Bartelli, who stared blankly back at her. Dinah's eyes itched and her throat burned. She shifted her sore wrists and heard something small clatter softly against the ground. She looked down and squinted at it. A fingernail. Dr. Bartelli walked over to it, the clicking of her low heels echoing against the floor again. She squatted low to pick it up, held it close to her face to scrutinize it, then sighed heavily as she remained crouched and looking up at Dinah, who maintained a look of outright hatred in her eyes.

"You're falling apart right before my eyes," Dr. Bartelli shook her head. "This shows me you were partially telling the truth, but the rest of your tale won't do. I'm certain that whatever your condition is, it's affected your mental faculties as well. If I understand you clearly, you expect us to believe in your magical water and some sort of...mermen? When really, this super-water you somehow managed to produce or steal is now a part of nothing more than an old-fashioned trade war— or a new-fangled arms race. Either way, my clients plan to win it, so you better start making some fucking sense."

I'd spit at this bitch if I had any saliva to spare, Dinah seethed.

Dr. Bartelli gently patted Dinah's right cheek and offered an apologetic look. Then, put the nail in one pocket of her lab coat and retrieved a phone from another. As she walked away from Dinah and toward the double-doored exit, Dinah could hear her hushed conversation, punctuated by the clicking of her heels against the linoleum.

"Don't alert the client just yet...but yes, the payload looks as if it's compromised," Dr. Bartelli continued. Then, nonchalantly, "That's what I planned to do—at least she'll be of some use that way."

Just before she went through the double doors, the doctor paused and waved a hand in the air. The gesture was immediately answered by a series of clicks. Suddenly, the wall in front of Dinah was polka-dotted in red. Dinah gulped hard, squeezed her eyes shut, and waited for the staccato of gunfire.

The first gunshot was met with a series of swears, then sounds of struggle. Since most of the men had been posted near the door, Dinah could make out little of what was happening until two of the men went crashing against the surgical tables and other equipment in the northeast corner of the room. Then, several more shots.

Suddenly, Dinah felt her entire body seize. She cried out in pain and slid from the chair. Every inch of her needed water—*her* water. Bullets whizzed overhead, and a helmet went crashing into the wall in front of her, but Dinah could do nothing to protect herself. She curled into a fetal position, her extremities wilting as her left gills pressed painfully against the cold linoleum. Her vision blurred, but she could make out the outline of a guard's boots near her face. The figure crouched low, his weapon in hand.

Please...kill me, Dinah couldn't say the words, or mouth them, so she thought them and fought to convey her last request to the guard using only her eyes.

But the guard was either oblivious to her expression or callous to it because he ignored her and gently placed his weapon on the ground. Then, he pulled back the sleeve of the black, calico shirt and revealed a marking on his inner wrist. Dinah squinted at it, but it was no use; it was too blotchy for her eyes to decipher.

"Hurry it up—she'll be back any minute!" A nearby voice pleaded.

The guard nearest her ignored that too. From her position on the floor, Dinah could see very little of his upper body movements. Then, at last, her vision failed her completely. Rough hands shoved something into her mouth and cupped it shut, forcing her to swallow. But there wasn't enough saliva, so the object slipped onto the floor.

"Shit!" A gruff voice said. "Get me a vial over here right now!"

Dinah felt her head being tipped backward, then the crisp, distinct taste of pure water. She swallowed and coughed, saliva swelling in her mouth for the first time in hours. Her voice was still too hoarse to speak, so she nodded feebly, and the gloved hand pressed several capsules into her mouth between short sips from a bejeweled glass vial attached to a dark green lanyard. Suddenly, Dinah's fingertips itched, and her body felt hot. She pushed herself up into a seated position and realized that everything around her had regained its definition, sharper than before. She cleared her throat and looked at the face of the man before her. He had a square jaw, ruddy complexion, sandy hair, and a lean, muscular body. She looked down at the exposed wrist that he had tried to show her moments before and recognized it instantly.

"An Inner Azimeth arc," Dinah said, her eyes wide.

"Yes," the guard said as he placed the vial around her neck. "And this is courtesy of Gideon. He left it with us out of fear that he'd been compromised. Drink. We've informed the elders of what transpired here today, and your orders are clear. You've been summoned to plant the Azimeth Arc and return."

Yes, Dinah let the contents of the vial course through her. Finally.

The itch in her fingers and toes began to subside, and Dinah looked down to see what had caused it; her nails had fully regrown. She could feel both hearts inside her thumping hard, pressing blood to each part of her dehydrated, withering body until she felt imbued with newfound strength. She plucked the dark brown contacts from her eyes and flicked them away, revealing the amethyst beneath. Her hair-tie snapped, and her hair surged forth from her scalp and tumbled free; kinky and dense until it draped to her breasts. She stood, shed her clothes, and belted a cry older than algae, man, and war, but not older than water.

The two guards looked at each other and nodded solemnly. The one who had been guarding the door had removed his helmet, revealing chestnut skin and a chiseled, radiant face framed with a full beard. Both remained solemnly by as she roared, as was the way of Inner Azimeth men when they heard their sirens' war cries. When she had finished, she nodded at them, and they resumed their battle stances.

"What the fuck is going on in here—" Dr. Bartelli burst through the double doors, scanned the room, then turned on her heels to run, but Dinah was too fast.

She spun her around and delivered a powerful kick to her chest. The wiry woman's body sailed through the air and collided with a guard running toward the lab, sending them both to the ground in a heap. He quickly recovered, glanced at Dinah, and reached for his walkie-talkie, trembling with fear. A voice crackled from the other end, but Dinah didn't give the guard a chance to respond. She ran full speed toward him until he dropped the walkie and drew his weapon, but she didn't falter or slow down. Instead, she shrieked so fiercely that the man screamed and fell to his knees. The lights in the narrow corridor flickered and burst from the intensity of the sound. Placards and other framed accolades vibrated violently until they slipped from the walls, and an alarm wailed in the distance as the wounded guard hemorrhaged from his ears and slumped onto the floor.

The water from the vial is from the deepest sanctum, Dinah thought calmly as she tore through a group of guards, ripping their weapons from their hands and bludgeoning her way through each corridor in search of an exit. *It's not just pure—it's imbued with memory. Gideon says this Chimera Program is done, and I won't mourn it. This place, with its rotten people and poisoned water, will never intermingle with us without destroying us in the process. I see that now.*

Each bone that fractured during combat healed quickly, and Dinah felt more powerful with each blow she delivered. Her mind was the sharpest it had been in months, and she felt an almost erotic pleasure pulsate in her as she mowed down everyone who stood in her way. For her, her path and instructions were clear: make it to the closest body of water, summon the Azimuth Arc to the surface, and dole out a punishment befitting a people who dealt in broken promises, deception, and murder.

The weapon, named for its place of origin, was considered so powerful that the elder Agarthans referred to it as 'The Renewer' in their ancient texts. All her life, she had feared it; Agarthans feared it too. Only surface dwellers had scoffed at its existence.

Dinah had learned long ago that there was once a time that Agarthans had shared it with humans. When she was little, she heard stories about how, in the beginning, life on the planet existed as three factions: Agarthans, Atlanteans, and Earthians—surface dwellers. For many years, they took turns hosting the Azimuth Arc as a gesture to maintain the checks and balances between them.

Then, one surface dweller asked to use it, but only did so to flood the world and remake it so that it bent to his prophecy. It worked. When those waters subsided, Agarthans collected the relic from the surface dwellers for good, but it was already too late. Some surface dwellers were already hailing the man as a miracle worker, allied with God. They began to form a religion around his deed and his story endured for millennia, void of any mention of Atlanteans and Agarthans. Many years after that, surface dwellers forgot about the original trifecta altogether, and the duties they had agreed upon to keep the balance.

They continued to poison the water, and as a result, Atlanteans' numbers dwindled nearly to extinction until Agarthans intervened. Dinah remembered her own parents, fretting over the amount of water that Agarthans had to expend to keep the Earthians and Atlanteans alive; the only reason the endeavor lasted as long as it did was that one drop of water from Agartha could purify a thousand gallons of surface water, and a drop of water taken from the innermost waters—an area they called the Inner Azimuth, could purify a million gallons.

By the time Agartha had decided that it could spare no more of its water, Dinah was of age to join their new effort to restore balance to the water: the Chimera Program. Observing that their allyship wasn't strong enough, Agarthans and Atlanteans reasoned that their best course was to intermingle with the surface dwellers until they produced offspring that would adopt some of their innate sensibilities. So, they launched the program with a group of genetically altered Agarthans.

Dinah nearly died during the ordeal, which required that she remain in aquatic stasis until she was endowed with every characteristic that would allow her to thrive in water, and on land. Then, she and those like her were dispatched to the surface to mingle, reproduce, and lead the surface dwellers to a better way.

As Dinah laid eyes on the exit to the lab, she pulled a lab coat over her bare body and was inwardly thankful that she hadn't shed her shoes. She opened the doors and saw that they let out onto a large parking lot. In the distance, she could see an overpass with signs headed north to D.C.

Virginia, Dinah buttoned the lab coat and looked for the quickest way out. *Too far to travel on foot dressed like this. I'm covered in blood. I need directions, and a car.*

She considered breaking a window, but noticed that some lab workers, likely evening shift employees, were weaving their way across the parking lot, key cards in hard.

I have to get out of here before the next wave sees the mess in there—or at least before the crew manning the security system calls in the cavalry. Dinah looked around once more, suppressing panic.

"Here!" the undercover Chimera Agent called to her from his place near the exit.

Dinah looked at the fresh purple wound on his reddish face and immediately knew why he was staying behind.

"I'll have to say you worked me over and took my keys," he tossed them to her but didn't move from where he stood, taking advantage of the security camera's blind spot.

Dinah caught the keys and pressed the alarm button. Minutes later, she was in the car and on her way to the closest place she knew to summon the Azimuth Arc. She tucked the vial around her neck into the bloodstained lab coat, took the exit, and sped toward the National Harbor.

***

Dinah pulled into a parking lot and popped the trunk. She sifted through the miscellaneous items until she found an old, checkered shirt, several sizes too big. As she swapped it out with the lab coat, she heard voices. A group of girls rounded the corner, talking excitedly and carrying posters scrawled with various slogans about ending climate change.

Too little, too late, kiddos, Dinah mused as she slammed the trunk and headed for the docks. She walked toward the Ferris wheel at the far edge of the dock, bought a ticket, and waited.

She avoided looking at the families around her and instead focused on the water. After consuming the contents of the vial, her sense of smell had heightened tenfold, and the water smelled rancid. Dinah looked out at the brown water and the happy, oblivious surface dwellers flocking to its edge, taking pictures in front of it as if it were something to behold, and her hands shook with rage. All around her, there was plastic. People sipped from straws and carried plastic bags, tossed plastic refuse over the sides of their boats when they were sure no one was looking.

I'm sick of it all, Dinah grunted as she stepped inside the car.

When the attendant closed its gate and moved to board the next batch of passengers, Dinah rested her hand on the windowsill of the car and waited for it to ascend. When it had reached its highest point, she undid the emergency hatch and climbed on top of the car, which wobbled violently as she did.

From up that high, Dinah could see miles of contaminated water in each direction. She heard people screaming below and felt the jolt from the brakes as the operator halted the ride, but she ignored it all. Dinah took a brief sip from the vial around her neck, crouched low so that her fingertips grazed the top of the car, and shrieked.

The stampede began instantly. People fled the docks and moved toward the man-made shore nearby. Those on the Ferris wheel with her tried to cry out to the operator below, but no one could function in the midst of her siren song. Dinah concentrated hard, pushing the notes from her belly the way a true Agarthan would. She felt her gills contract taking in air just as her lungs felt depleted.

Dinah escalated the octave of her call, letting her voice undulate. She shut her eyes and clenched her fists and pushed the sound outward until she could feel it reaching into the water, reaching beneath the poisoned depths, through the portal point, and into the sacred hollow she called her home. Reaching until, at long last, it pulled the Azimuth Arc from its hidden place and out from desecrated waters that surrounded one of the most powerful cities in the surface dwellers' world. Birds scattered, sirens wailed below, but she did not stop until she opened her eyes and saw the first ripples on the water.

It's coming, Dinah collapsed and nearly slid from the top of the car, but she held onto the spokes that cradled the car between its drive rims and steadied herself, waiting.

The arc burst from the waves and blasted upward into the air. It stopped in mid-air once it reached Dinah, then sat itself down on the top of the car. Dinah shrank from it before realizing what she was doing, then considered that she had never seen it before and would likely never see it again. It was a half-dome made of golden light, protruding from a flat platform of perpetual lightning that had been flattened razor thin. It vibrated with energy, and golden waves rippled gently within its globe. The ripples sounded like echoes of the ocean, distorted and hypnotic.

Dinah crouched down again, slowly. *This is the part that's trickiest,* she wiped sweat from her brow and extended her hand. *It only has two commands…expand, or collapse.*

Though Dinah had never laid eyes on the Azimuth before, its simple choices made sense to her.

Whoever fashioned this knew us well, Dinah nodded to herself. *They knew that no matter how little we know about the universe, we are at least able to observe that there are only two things it requires of itself, and all its participants. Everything here—and everywhere—expands, and collapses, contracting into itself. Just two choices, and I have one to make. Do I expand the waters, swelling and drowning these miserable beings and all their progress, as the ancient surface dweller did once before? Or do I collapse it into the Azimuth and leave them with a barren wasteland?*

Her fingertips grazed against the Azimuth, and she felt its power and prompting. She needed to choose. She reached for it again, ready to command it. Then, she heard a sound.

It was a whimper coming from below. A child.

"I don't know, sweetheart, but it's going to be alright."

No, no, NO! Dinah's anger fought for sovereignty over the rest of her thoughts. *Don't listen to them. This is what they do. They ignore every warning until a calamity reaches them, then they cower, beg for time, and offer more false promises. Either drown them or let them scorch, but you need to choose now.*

Dinah squeezed her eyes shut again, but that only opened her ears to the cries of the passengers below even more. She forced herself to harden, and return the same, cold indifference they had shown her over the years. She wrapped herself in it and blotted out their pleas, reaching instead for the arc. Dinah could see her reflection in it now—the round cheeks, high forehead, and crown of deep brown helixes that framed her frowning face. In the face staring back at her, she saw in her a connection, a kinship to the first female surface dwellers. Things could possibly have been different if they had continued to rule the outer rim.

Those women knew water, Dinah suddenly remembered her mother's stories about how all tribes held water sacred when the outer surface was one big land. *They warred for it, walked miles for it, gave offerings for it, and held it on their heads so that it did not spill. They took only what they needed from it and were grateful for what it gave. Those women—those people—knew water and guarded it as fiercely as they guarded their own future.*

Dinah took a deep breath and laid a palm on the Azimuth. Everyone gasped and whispered as she did, because outwardly, she had begun to float in the air with the arc rising with her as if it was tethered to her outstretched hand. But Dinah noticed none of it. The weightlessness, her feet skimming the ground, and her hair floating wildly like a gathering storm cloud; she felt none of it, because her mind had been transported inside the Azimuth Arc.

Inside, there were only golden waves. The waves were the horizon, sun, and shore. As they lapped at her feet, she felt the waves present a choice she hadn't considered. They whispered to her that the third choice was one used at the beginning of time, too old for Agarthans, Atlanteans, and surface-dwelling Earthians to comprehend. Then, it showed her the third choice. She could see it clearly, though its image appeared only as a mirage on the waves dancing at her feet. As she comprehended the third choice, she chose it in her heart, but her mind swelled with other questions, and her lips moved to ask them.

Where did you come from?

Who used the Azimuth Arc first?

Are you a machine?

Are you…a god?

The Azimuth suppressed the last two words so that Dinah's lips moved but no sound escaped, and its golden waves deepened to crimson. Dinah stopped talking, and the waves shifted from red to orange, then back to their original hue of gold. Then, the arc prompted her, once more, to choose.

Choose, or return.

Dinah felt something hot strike the left shoulder of her physical body.

It feels like…I'm running out of time.

Another sharp blow to her physical body, this time to her left side.

She moved her lips to deliver her answer and found that her speech had been returned to her. "I choose the seal," Dinah closed her eyes as she said the words, and when she opened them, she found that the world had abruptly snapped back into view around her.

She remained suspended in mid-air for a moment, then crashed into the top of the steel car with a thud. Her ankle snapped, and she cried out in pain, but she gritted her teeth and willed it to heal. As her ankle bone reformed itself, she touched her hand to another wound and withdrew it with a hiss. Blood leaked from her shoulder and side, where two bullets had gone straight through, but she had no time to focus on those wounds because the ground had begun to shake.

People screamed and opened the emergency hatches on their Ferris wheel cars to wave their hands at the helicopters flying overhead. The Azimuth Arc emitted a low, humming sound, then propelled itself down into the water, sending nearby boats careening from the force of its impact. The sun had set during the commotion, and the helicopter overhead turned its floodlights on, blinding her. A man yelled demands through a bullhorn, as another beside him trained his weapon on her.

Too many sounds…too many surface dwellers, a calm washed over Dinah. She reached to unbutton the oversized shirt and another bullet burned its way through her shoulder. *They're not trying to kill me. They've seen me float, heal myself, and summon what they probably believe is a bioweapon. This means they've been ordered to take me alive again. But…they're much too late for that.*

Dinah removed her shoes, walked to the edge of the Ferris wheel car, and looked around. The sirens, man on the bullhorn, and bleating of the helicopter wings against the sky swirled into white noise. She tented her arms above her head, closed her eyes, and dove into the water.

As she plummeted downward, she thought of what she had done and what it would cost her people. All the chimera agents would have to go into hiding and live out their last days on whatever supply of capsules they'd saved, because now there was no way for them to go home again.

Dinah had heard the wailing children. She'd seen the young, naïve girls, giddy in their optimism for the future of the surface, their home. She had cared for ill surface dwellers who'd flocked into the emergency room daily, ignorant that their water was the reason for their increased sickness, pestilence, and death, and decided not to punish them because they were already punishing themselves enough.

But I didn't reward them either, Dinah smiled triumphantly as her body struck the water. *I chose the seal.*

The earth quaked that day, and everyone dismissed the tremor as an unexpected seismic event. They would never know that beneath their feet, the Azimuth Arc had sealed their water off from Agartha and Atlantis, leaving a pathway between them but no way for surface dwellers to pass. Since Atlantis shared the surface dweller's water, the arc merely expanded, closed itself around the ancient aquatic city, and hardened, walling its inhabitants off from the poisoned water.

Dinah perished knowing that she had chosen the right answer, even though it was one steeped in sacrifice, and as her submerged body disintegrated in the toxic waves, the vial slipped from her neck and purified the water around her so that everyone around her could see, and finally understand.

The change in the water was instant, and it bloomed outward from her floating body until everyone who stood on the docks of the harbor could see it. When they did, they all gasped. The water had become clear. Within minutes, a crowd had formed on the patch of man-made beach near the Ferris wheel. For the first time ever, they could see through the depths of the water, all the way down to the bottom. The refuse was still there, even more visible than before, and people gazed at the scores of things they discarded.

Murmurs went up from the crowd. The girls who Dinah had seen in the parking lot made their way through until they stood at the water's edge. They looked at each other and began removing their shoes. They swiped at anything they could reach until a woman from a nearby restaurant ran over to them, pulling gloves from the pocket of her apron and passing them around. A brown veil had hidden their accumulated filth from them, and in the span of one sunset, Dinah had lifted it. It was the only legacy she could leave, and it would have to be enough.

"It appears that a strange occurrence at the National Harbor has—get this, folks—turned back the contamination clock on the D.C. area watershed. If you look at the footage captured by the Metropolitan Police chopper earlier this evening, you can see a figure diving into the water. A few minutes after she goes under, the water around her turns clear for miles. Donny—have you ever seen anything like this in all your reporting years?"

"I've been taking samples from the harbor since before the project was finished, and even I can't explain what happened here tonight…the water is clear, straight to the bottom! I've already taken a small sample, and there's nothing I can compare it to at the moment…."

"*We're here live with some of the residents who were actually on that Ferris wheel with what appeared to be a mentally ill woman talking into a glowing device of some kind. Did she threaten any of you? Were you able to determine what was happening from inside the ride?*'

"*She didn't threaten anyone or anything. I guess it was scary when she started to float—*"

"*Started to float?*"

"*Yes…err…anyway, it was all pretty powerful.*"

"*Well folks, there you have it. Some strange events took place on the water today.*"

Chimera Agent

Dahlia's Island

Sweat stung Dahlia's eyes as she worked, rolling from her disheveled hairline then streaking down her dirty face, pooling at the philtrum of her lips. She glanced at the sky and made a mental note of the sun's position to monitor the time. She had to work quickly to convert the volleyball pump into a pressurized weapon, and she was already moving slowly because she paused at every step to check that a component had been properly reattached, and sometimes, to break down in tears.

Her tawny skin was covered in grit, and there was sand and debris mangled into the high bun of braids atop her head, but her hands were still clean. She'd used the last bit of her water to wash the sticky blood from her hands so she could craft the device without her sticky fingers impeding the task. She fought the urge to wipe the sweat from her eyes as her shaky hands poured the last of the salt from the makeshift pantry in their tent, and any other seasoning that contained salt, into a tiny hole she'd hammered into the side of the small aluminum pump. After plugging it with a sturdy twig, she held the pump at eye level and pulled the lever out as far as it could go. Then she jammed it forward with full force, producing a spray of salt. Success.

If jellyfish are anything like slugs, this should slow them down, Dahlia reasoned as she tucked the modified pump into the back of her shorts. *And I'm not leaving here without that sample.*

She glanced at the sky once more, this time longer than before. Once, at a time that now felt as if it was eons ago, she would've taken time to gaze at the brilliant panoramic view, admiring its layers of colors that bled delicately into each other. The periwinkle-orange tones of an encroaching dusk used to be her favorite sight in the world. She and Brian had spent their last spring break at the beach, and she loved to grab his hand, and they'd both kick off their shoes and wade into the water, leaving a trail of clothes behind them. Now, the movement of the sinking sun served her only in that it marked the time, and from the look of it at that moment, Dahlia knew she had just a few previous minutes left to run.

Just an hour before, she'd dropped her walkie-talkie against the rocks during her frenzied sprint away from the carnage. Right before then, Elias, her team's chopper pilot, and project lead, told her that she had to make it back to their original drop point within the next two hours if she wanted to have any chance of being rescued.

"DAHLIA," Elias' voice had come through loud and scratchy, just moments before her walkie fell and shattered against the rocks. "DO YOU READ ME? HOW MANY ARE WE BRINGING BACK? MED TEAM NEEDS TO KNOW."

Dahlia could barely make out what he said over the sounds of people yelling orders in the background.

"WHAT?" she yell-whispered through the walkie, hoping he'd heard her. He had.

"HOW MANY?" Elias must've moved away from the loud flying machines because Dahlia could hear him clearly. In a way, it was worse. While he was yelling and straining his voice, it had been hard for Dahlia to discern whether the tone he was using denoted a routine sense of urgency or fear. Now, she could hear that it was fear.

"Just me," Dahlia was surprised at how small her own voice sounded in the moment, even in a silence filled only by the sound of balmy wind rustling the tops of the trees deeper inland and the thumping of her own heart in her ears. She tried again, yelling over the madness on his side, "IT'S JUST ME— ROGER IS MISSING AND THE OTHERS ARE...THEY'RE GONE."

There was a brief pause before Elias yelled into the walkie again. "WELL," Elias came in crackly but audible once more, "WE'LL CIRCLE ROUND AS MANY TIMES AS WE CAN.

YOU JUST GET TO THAT PAD, COPY?"

"COPY," Dahlia's voice cracked as she belted her reply. She'd have to get moving toward the cave; she'd already made too much noise.

Dahlia pressed her back against the gypsum walls of the cave as she continued to heel-toe herself on the narrow ledge that led to its mouth. Once she made it to a space wide enough for her to make a full turn, she'd be able to climb down and stay low. The slurping sounds were behind her now; logically, she knew that. But the wet, sickening pops of bones snapping echoed in the cavernous space and managed to crawl into her eardrums even as she moved further away and into the light.

If she didn't have to keep her palms against the walls of the cave for balance, she would've clapped them over her ears to drown it out, but the handholds and footholds along the wall had become sparser as she inched forward, so she ignored the noises and tried to focus on the strategic placement of each coming step.

She squinted against the sun. It was getting dangerously low in the sky and casting lengthy shadows along the sand where the jungle at the island's center faded into its perimeter of picturesque beach. Her clothes were in tatters, and she'd lost a shoe to the Feeders, but all she had to do now was get the helicopter pad. There, a chopper loaded with supplies for six people would unexpectedly discover they'd be heading back to

Virginia with a surplus of unused meds because only she'd survived.

That's wishful thinking, Dahlia. She carefully placed one foot, then the next. *You haven't survived anything just yet.*

Of the four Clermont High seniors and two Hudson High seniors chosen to research the sandy biome, all but Dahlia had met their gruesome end. She'd watched all but two of them perish since Roger was technically still missing. But at this point, Dahlia was certain he'd met the same fate.

Roger and Becca, the two other students who'd been chosen along with Dahlia and Brian, hadn't been friends with Dahlia beforehand. They'd taken some of the same advanced classes and knew most of the same people, but since Dahlia had transferred to Clermont in her junior year after her mom moved to Fredericksburg for a promotion, she hadn't had a chance to make many friends at all. She didn't mind it as much in the beginning because the coursework at Clermont was tougher than her last school and her studying kept her preoccupied, but over time she felt the sting of isolation every time a school function was announced, and she had no one to sit or talk with. Even striking up conversations in the cafeteria had felt like a game of musical chairs at Clermont—every time she saw a group of students who looked like they'd warm up to her, it never lasted long. Eventually, it became clear that every space she thought she'd fit in had already been filled.

Only Brian had gone out of his way to be nice.

Then, after months of hard work with Brian as her lab partner, she'd won a spot on the research trip. The school called an assembly to announce the winners, and students filed in excitedly, Dahlia included. But just a few moments later, Dahlia had realized that the memory would be bittersweet for her; as soon as the principal announced her name with the other students, she heard other students whispering angrily about it.

"How'd she win?"

"Didn't she just transfer here?"

"And didn't she come from that shitty school on the south side?"

Dahlia remembered how numb she became after that day, but in that moment, their words had stung more than the salty mingle of tears and sweat that blurred her vision as she maneuvered her way to the helicopter pad.

Dahlia knew that she'd have to move quickly. Not because of the monsters' speed, but because they were everywhere. Moving, smelling, and adapting to the movements of their prey. Dahlia had seen their transparent bodies blend in with leaves, water, and sand so far, and the darker it got, the easier it was for them to do.

Think, Dahlia. *Double-check everything and make sure you're smarter than they are—smarter than those damn Feeders.*

"Feeders."

Brian had called them that on their first day there. As soon as they'd set up their camp for later, they'd all grabbed their gear and cameras and headed out with the hope of discovering something noteworthy enough to secure funding and scholarships for years to come. As Dahlia predicted, her Clermont peers clustered together, and the Hudson students went off on their own. But none of them knew that they didn't have years left to research anything, or that from that point on, all except Dahlia had a few precious hours left to live.

Now they're all gone, Dahlia replayed the gory scene in her mind as she ran to a nearby tree. *I don't understand how it happened so quickly.*

They'd found the mutilated bodies of the two students from Hudson together, when the four of them were still a group. Their group had been vigilant that night, setting simple animal traps around their camp and taking care to pack away their food at night. They'd done everything their group had done, yet it hadn't been enough.

"Yeesh," Roger whistled when he saw them, which made Dahlia shudder. "Evan and Gemma, was it? Poor fuckers got worked over pretty bad. Guess they won't be winning any research dollars for the great Hudson High."

He chuckled, and Brian snapped.

"Are you really joking right now?" Brian's face had flushed red as he got closer to Roger until they were standing nose to nose. "They're dead, and we don't even know what the hell did this to them."

"Brian's right," Dahlia had tried to step between them, but Roger had moved her aside without bothering to look at her. Instead, he kept his eyes locked on Brian, seemingly determined to show her and Becca that he wasn't deterred by their four-inch difference in height.

She'd been annoyed by how forcefully he'd moved her aside, but she'd continued to reason with them both from a few feet away as Becca stood farther, nervously shuffling her feet with her arms crossed in front of her chest as she avoided looking at anything in particular.

"Look at this?" Dahlia had pleaded, motioning toward the corpses as she suppressed the urge to vomit. "Whatever did this was able to attack both of them with all their traps set, and without us even hearing it. We need to figure out what it was so we don't end up dead before the week is out. In fact, I think we should call this in now."

Camouflaged in enough sand or leaves to cover her quaking body, she witnessed the gruesome awe of the creatures' work first-hand as Feeders consumed the last of the Hudson students. Each monster had dissolved each large chunk of flesh slowly over the course of nearly a day. Crouched behind a rock, she'd cupped her own mouth and gulped back tears as she watched them. Dahlia's only relief was that she'd gotten beyond tears quickly because she knew she couldn't afford the blurred vision or sting of the salt on her face, already abraded from her wiping the tears from her face with the back of her gritty, sand-speckled hands.

Dahlia bit her lip at the thought and her mouth flooded with the metallic taste of her own blood. She tried to swallow but found that the simple motion was painful since her mouth was completely void of saliva. Her head pounded furiously, throbbing mercilessly behind her eyes. She instinctively knew that all of it was the result of dehydration and overall heat exhaustion. It had been such a long time since she'd experienced it that severely, that she was sure the last time had been when she ignored her track coach's instructions about water intake for her first meet. She'd never done it again after that.

Well, at least not willingly, Dahlia took a deep breath and focused on trying to breathe through her nose more to slow the sticky, parched feeling blooming in her throat.

The appendages of her travel group lay in frothy piles near the back of the shallow cave they'd all thought it wise to hide in just a few hours before, and their personal effects were strewn over the rocks leading into it. A taupe shoulder bag. A hat. Boots that Roger had repeatedly reminded them cost him a few hundred bucks because they were "designed for rugged terrain."

Perhaps they had been. Even mired in the sandy dirt of the cave, they still looked pretty durable from where she stood.

"Maybe they don't like dark meat either, which is crazy to me because it's always moist from what I hear."

That was the macabre, hurtful joke Roger made after the Feeders gutted their entire group by half, seizing Becca first after the two Hudson students, and leaving Dahlia, Brian and Roger behind. She had ignored it the same way she'd ignored his distasteful jokes about what she had to do to earn her seat on the coveted research expedition. *"No way you passed those tests. I'm supposed to believe you learned the same stuff at your old school? Didn't you guys have metal detectors there?"*

She ignored his jabs about Brian's affection for her, too. She even tolerated the monkey emojis he posted after each of her comments in the group text Becca had established for them to share research notes before the trip.

"We made it, guys! Crazy how we all got accepted. First team out, too...so anything I find is getting named after me. Ha. No hard feelings, though."

Becca had been Roger's opposite right up until she died—welcoming, upbeat, and pleasant to be around. Dahlia used to marvel at her optimism but always understood it. What did she Becca have to be despondent over? She was wealthy, savvy, ambitious, and liked. Dahlia looked around the cave for anything that belonged to Becca. She saw one soiled shoe and a few clumps of long brown hair still attached to mounds of scalp. One mound still had a hair clip in it. Dahlia leaned over and tried to wretch, but nothing came out. She tasted bile in the back of her throat. She wanted nothing more than to scream as loud as her lungs would allow, but she wiped the back of her mouth and moved forward instead.

Dahlia tried to block the rest of her thoughts about Becca out of her mind but couldn't forget that as kind as she was, her opinion of Becca had still soured shortly after they all stepped foot on the island. Becca had been tall and slender with large green eyes. Roger had been trying to get her attention even before the trip, but it was never Roger that she wanted.

"I just really hope I hook up with someone nice on this trip, you know?" Becca admitted the first night they broke camp.

At that point, Dahlia had given her confession little thought. Then, after it was clear that they were being hunted by the creatures on the island, Dahlia watched Becca try to latch onto Brian in any way that she could. During one escape, she'd held onto his arm so tightly as they ran from an encroaching group of Feeders that she caused him to stumble a bit.

"Hey!" Dahlia had hissed at Becca as quietly as she could. "Could you knock it off for one second? You're gonna make him fall, and the noise is gonna get us all killed."

They'd stared at each other intensely for a few moments, and then Becca had sulked away, making sure to stay a few paces ahead of them all.

Dahlia keenly remembered all the other times Becca had touched his arm and drawn him away from the group for secretive conversations during the trip, too, though she felt guilty for thinking of it at all.

I know she tried to get close to him, Dahlia swiped at a mosquito and almost lost her balance. *It doesn't mean she was a bad person. If anything, it made her a lot like you. Who wouldn't try to get close to someone in all this?*

She tried to stay focused on her surroundings as she darted from cover to cover and found that the maneuver helped her gain ground quickly. *It didn't do either of us any good, though. Becca is gone, liquefied to pulp at this point...and I'll be finished too if I don't get to the chopper."*

As her breaths pushed out into the humidity in short, painful bursts, she continued to sprint. Her thoughts pivoted to Becca again and Dahlia let them. She knew it was just her brain's way of preventing her from having a meltdown, but she resented it, nonetheless. She would've sighed if she wasn't winded from running. She grunted in frustration instead.

What she thought of this time was how Becca hadn't been wearing the right shoes. The dainty flats she wore against all their advice—and against the written guidelines they'd all received in a dossier before they left—were no match for the mangled network of roots and bushes that carpeted the floor of the island's jungle. Once she fell, the feeders swarmed, and they couldn't look back. No one had even dared.

Shoes, Dahlia's mind grasped for something to block out the memory of the sound of Feeders slurping Becca's sun-kissed skin from her legs. *Think about shoes. Remember that joke Brian made about shoes? Boots, I think...*

"Feeders don't like boot leather, so, maybe they don't like vegans either, since I'm sure that's what you guys taste like," Brian had chuckled nervously as he whispered the joke to her just a few hours before. Dahlia tried to not to think about the desperate look in his eye as he did.

Her brain wrapped around the grim humor of Brian's joke and white-knuckled it for sanity. She thought of the boot and forced herself not to think of its wearer, who was currently being consumed just feet below her. The boot's leather appeared to be harder to break down than mounds of flesh partially coated in areas of what had—just hours before—been youthful skin.

Brian's skin.

Dahlia's mind somersaulted and, despite her staunchest effort, landed on a memory of Brian's face. If he'd lived, he would've told them stories and jokes like the one he'd made about the boots to ease the tension in that moment, as they sat around a fire. He would've sat next to her with a beer in his left hand, kicking his foot forward at certain points in the story to punctuate his off-color humor. If he'd lived, he would've been laughing and smiling even as he told the horrific tale. She tried to picture that smile and remember his embrace, but her mind could only conjure what she imagined most—what his half-consumed face looked like among the other liquefied mounds on the floor of the cave. She shuddered.

Then, she slipped.

The universe around her glitched and cast all her years of athletic muscle memory and balance aside as she slipped and fell to the rocky surface below.

As she cautiously slid herself up on her elbows, her mind raced. Had they seen her? As she angled her neck toward their gruesome feeding, she noticed that she'd narrowly missed cracking her skull on a jagged rock jutting from the ground behind her and that one of the Feeders was still for a long moment. Then, with no noise to confirm its suspicion, it again shifted its body over a pile of dismembered flesh, undulating on it as its carpal suckers worked to slurp at the remains. Dahlia hated the way it seemed to enjoy it, its movements mimicking the gentle thrusts and arches of an intimate act.

The rhythm of it made Dahlia think of Brian and her stomach lurched at the perverseness of her own mind. Sex and death. Consumption and death. Consumption and sex and death. The sickening thoughts flickered rapidly as a zoetrope as she struggled to her feet.

Suddenly, the sound of a helicopter washed the thoughts away and flooded her body with adrenaline. The monsters rose to their feet, too, unfolding themselves up and open as if they'd just awakened from a long night's sleep. But they were too slow. Dahlia pulled her tank top off and jabbed her hands inside the pockets of her jean shorts for the two lighters. Her vision blurred with tears as she broke the larger one and dumped its contents onto her shirt and the ground around it before using the other to set it ablaze.

Goodbye, Brian.

I'm sorry, Becca.

Fuck you, Roger.

Dahlia ran from the wall of fire and toward the sound of the helicopter. The thud of its wings blotted out the noise around it as it descended toward the pad. Her arms burned, but she kept flailing them wildly as she ran, afraid that she'd be overlooked; forgotten. Pain sprinted up her sides and her calves burned. Her breath huffed out in short, violent bursts as her body warred with her mind, urging it to quit. But still, she moved forward to the makeshift pad, a red sheet they'd sprayed with a giant white "x" and anchored to the ground near the shore, shortly after landing.

When she reached the edge of the sheet, she collapsed to

her hands and knees, panting and tearful with the makeshift weapon at her side. The sound of the chopper wrung the sound from the air, but she felt a gloved hand on her shoulder, and looked up to see a kind weathered face.

"Are you Dahlia?" He yelled his question over the noise. "I'm Elias. We spoke earlier. You look like you've been through the wringer. Let's get you home."

Dahlia nodded and climbed to her feet, dusting the sand from her knees. She walked toward the chopper with her sides still burning, and could hear Elias following behind. Thirst tightened her throat, and her blistered feet stung as she walked. As she prepared to climb in, she saw that the med techs had begun pointing and yelling. Dahlia squeezed her eyes shut, not wanting to turn around.

*I don't have anything left—whatever this is, I can't...*Dahlia turned, and saw that it wasn't a Feeder that had caused the commotion.

Three-fourths of Roger's face had been liquefied, mostly on the left side. His left eyeball dangled from the partially dissolved socket and the gumline of his mouth was also exposed, lipless, and oozing. Both of his legs were intact, but his left arm was covered in bubbly contusions that leaked blood and pus onto the sand. A clump of his ash-blonde hair was slipping into his eye, and he used his right hand to swat it away. It peeled off and landed near his bare feet in a hairy, wet clump. With his left arm, he restrained Elias by the neck.

"You know," Roger's eyes burned into Dahlia as he spoke, "I'm pretty sure that the only thing that kept me alive back there was that I couldn't just let you take all the credit for this discovery, especially knowing what I just sacrificed."

"Oh, my fucking god—is THAT what you're worried about right now?" Dahlia's exhaustion morphed into anger as she continued. "Let him go and get on the damn 'copter, Roger. You need a lot of medical treatment, and we don't have much time. You want credit? You got it. Take the goddamn Nobel Peace Prize, for all I care...but we need to go...NOW."

"You should listen to her," Elias pleaded.

"Shut up!" Roger tightened his grip. "You didn't let me finish! I said that's what kept me alive when I *thought* I was going to die.

But I'm not going to die, Dahlia. I'm transforming into whatever they are. I'm even starting to hear them. It's beautiful actually, it's—it's like this calm, persistent hunger to soak up all types of life. We consume plants, animals, humans, whatever we need."

"We?" Dahlia's face crumpled in confusion. "You're still you, Roger. There are medics in the chopper—they can save you if we leave now!"

Roger grinned, shedding more bits of his face. "I'm not going anywhere. All of you make for one hefty protein supply for the rainy season. So, none of you are leaving either."

That's when Dahlia saw them.

He was just wasting time, the realization washed over Dahlia slowly. *And now we're surrounded.*

Maintaining eye contact with Roger, Dahlia called over her shoulder to the medics, who were now huddled low in the chopper. "Is there a weapon on board?"

"Yeah!" A woman medic called out, her voice cracking with fear. "There's a flare gun and a few pistols here!"

"Good!" Dahlia said over her shoulder, eyes still glued on Roger. "You may need to use it."

"Okay," another medic called out with panic in his voice. "Whatever you're about to do, we need you to do it fast—we're burning gas here!"

In response, Dahlia took a deep breath and swallowed hard, forcing herself to suppress the pain from her bodily injuries. Then, she bent at the knees and rushed forward.

Sorry about this, Elias, Dahlia slammed into both men, knocking them off their feet. She landed atop the pile, then quickly rolled to recover the salt-gun she'd fashioned earlier.

"Get back to the helicopter, Elias," Dahlia grabbed him by the elbow and attempted to pull him up.

As he struggled to his feet, he nearly stumbled, then cried out in pain, "I—I can't! Something's got my ankle!"

Shit, Dahlia aimed at the Feeder that was swelling itself

around Elias' right calf. *I hope this works.*

Before she could fire a shot, Roger landed a blow to the side of her head that sent her spinning. She landed face-down in the hot sand and clamored to escape a Feeder that was closing in on her from behind. Blood spilled from her nose, and she spat red. Roger swung again, but she dodged it, instinctively protecting her already fragile nose. She scanned the ground for the salt-gun and found it near Elias, who was now seated on the sand and using his free left leg to push himself away from the Feeder. He whimpered once he discovered that sliding backward didn't loosen the Feeder's grip.

Dahlia watched as more of his leg absorbed into the deadly, gelatinous mass. She dove for the salt-gun and rained shots on Elias' nearly consumed leg. The Feeder shrank from the salt, and tendrils of white smoke hissed from the wound. Elias wriggled his leg free and ran toward the chopper without looking back. Roger circled her apprehensively.

"What's in that thing?" He pointed a marred index finger at the weapon.

"Come closer and find out" Dahlia glared at him.

I don't have enough salt to finish off all these Feeders, Dahlia continued glaring at Roger, trying her best to look fierce. *So, I hope he doesn't call my bluff.*

"You think I'm gonna let some diversity-hire student take

me down with a rickety salt-shaker?" Roger sneered, and the eyeball that had been dangling lost its battle with gravity. "Bitch!"

It hit the ground, dragging its sinewy tail behind it, and Dahlia's stomach lurched upward toward her throat. In that distracted moment, Roger swiped for the gun and Dahlia sidestepped him just in time. She aimed the salt-gun at his collapsing face and blasted it. He screamed and stumbled backward, cursing and swinging his fists blindly.

"Get her!" Roger screamed at the beings inching toward him. "Kill that bitch!"

"I don't think it works that way," Dahlia said quietly as she watched him suffer. "Right now, you're still human to them—which means you're still food. And since most are coming from the south shore at your back, they'll flock to you and eat the rest of you because you're a closer food source. Do you understand me, Roger? If you stay here...you'll die."

Dahlia felt tears well in her eyes as she felt the weight of each death she'd endured on the island settle over her. "So, I'll ask you this one more time; will you come with us?"

"Fuck you!" Roger continued to swing blindly. "I'm one of them! I'm transforming! You'll see!"

"No, Roger...I won't," Dahlia withdrew a test tube from her pocket and quickly scooped a salted, shriveled piece of Feeder into it before she turned and jogged toward the chopper.

With one hand, she shoved the wriggling, bottled specimen into her pocket. She used the other to shoot at any Feeder she saw in her peripheral as she went until she'd emptied all the salt from the pump.

She ran toward the medics, who frantically beckoned for her to climb into the hovering aircraft. Her feet struck the sand in tandem rhythm with her pounding heart. Her mind moved, almost as swiftly as her feet, to thoughts of water, rest, and home. Dahlia ran and ran and couldn't bear to look back and see Roger's face because she knew that even if he was telling the truth about the Feeders transforming his body, it still meant that he would die without experiencing the transformation he really needed—the one that would've let him run to safety with her.

The one that would've let him trust her enough to believe her when she told him that she didn't want to leave him behind.

Roger shrank in the distance as they gained altitude. She watched him until he became a speck on the light beige sand, then slumped in her seat as the medics checked her wounds and applied ointments and bandages. When they were finished, she pulled the test tube from her pocket, checked its seal, then watched its contents shift and bubble until it was still. Then she returned it to her pocket, adjusted her seat belt, and looked out at the waves beneath them. As her eyelids became heavy, she thought of the future she held in the palm of her hand moments ago, now tucked into her left pocket. She thought of the peers she'd lost, too. Then she thought of Brian and how he would've told the story of that day if he'd been there to see it, and a smile formed on her tear-streaked face as she imagined it.

"You should've seen her. She gave those Feeders hell! I told you she was bad-ass, Roger. I'm telling you guys—she's going places."

Magnets

Cherish stood hiding amidst the stuffed animals, soiled socks, and other clutter inside the closet of her childhood bedroom. There was a strange mixture of smells formed from the things that she had never bothered to remove. The cardboard shoeboxes full of old birthday cards and photo albums she'd stored on the narrow shelf space had not survived the leaks in the closet ceiling, so the stale smell of things clean and unclean mingled in her nose as she breathed as quietly as she could.

Her hair was still wet from the shower, and a loose braid had freed itself from her bun and was currently tickling the middle of her back. Cherish struggled not to flinch when a roach scuttled near her toe, the sliver of light from the closet door exposing its flat, brown exoskeleton in the dark. She suddenly felt a powerful yet fleeting hatred for the roach in that moment. She hated its freedom and aptitude for filth and terrain of all kinds. In contrast, almost every moment of her life that led up to this point had been shrouded with the type of warm familiarity that always bred naivety. Even more, she hated that she couldn't bear to crush the vermin beneath her bare foot because she couldn't stomach the sound of its plump body exploding into slimy fragments beneath her weight. She glanced at it briefly before gluing her eyes back to the bedroom door, watching for signs of Darren. Meanwhile, the pest crawled merrily away having escaped death at the hands one of its cruel, gargantuan gods.

Though her ankle seared with pain from her hasty retreat into her closet, Cherish focused on singling out every sound in her mother's apartment. She could hear the newscast blaring from the television speakers. She could hear Darren, her mother's boyfriend, as his heavy boots creaked along the thinly carpeted floorboards of their apartment. At that moment, the only thing to trump the thought of what would happen to her when he found her was fear of what had happened to her mother since the storm began. But Cherish steadied her breathing and willed her heart to beat slower so that she could make out more of the broadcast coming from her television just a few feet away. She peered through the crack in the door to make out as much of the broadcast as she could.

"Another strange phenomenon has been reported," said the news reporter.

He wore a windbreaker and a look of bewilderment as he stood in the midst of a ravaged area that appeared to be downtown. Cherish could see the National Monument behind him. Then, she could see something else behind him that was rising slowly into the air as he spoke. Cherish squinted at the object, which was a dark and greenish color. It spun faster and faster as it rose slowly into the air. When it had risen to a height where it was just behind the reporter's shoulder, Cherish could see that it was a fire hydrant.

"Reports of this peculiar event are now coming in from across the globe. Something appears to be affecting metal ob—," he continued, but television went dark before the jittery newscaster could finish his live report.

Then the whole apartment went dark, and Cherish suddenly realized she was cold. She'd stood in the closet for several minutes. Her body was void of water droplets or sweat now, and her skin was cool to the touch. The only thing she was keenly aware of was the way in which the absence of sound amplified her hearing. Now, she could hear Darren spouting drunken slurs as he lurched down the hallway. He was near her brother's room now, which was adjacent to hers. But Cherish knew her younger brother wasn't there.

Cherish and Darren was alone in her mother's apartment. Cramped and shabby as it was, the days Cherish spent visiting her mother Celia had brought a rhythm back into the life that she often missed since she set out on her own. Cherish, her mother and her younger brother Tyron had cultivated that rhythm for years. The modest meals cooked in their small kitchen, their time in front of the television watching their favorite shows as their mother braided or brushed their hair— it was all a rhythm they knew. And the routine of it all was held together by their quiet acceptance that Cherish and Tyron's father would never return. He'd slipped out of their lives as noiselessly as a flower closing its bloom, and they'd been left to contend with it as best they knew how.

Years had rolled by in this way. Cherish had grown tall and sharp and often drew praise from teachers on the consistency of her work and grades. And if she'd learned nothing else from her mother, it was that consistency and stability was the one thing she could cling to, much in the way that Celia did after her husband left her with two small children to fend for alone. Throughout her life, Cherish had come to admire the way her mother held down stable work and strove to maintain the standard of living that the family had enjoyed before they'd been abandoned but Cherish also saw that catering to them had also worn Celia down.

Both Celia and her mother stood just above 5'7, with long slender limbs that made even their smallest movements appear graceful. Both women had small, dark, almond shaped eyes. Their thick hair they kept braided or twisted and piled on their heads. Both had skin the color of caramel syrup, impossibly small hands, and long, narrow feet. Celia had always told her daughter that she loved dance when she was little and that it was in their blood because of the natural posture and balance they'd always possessed.

Though there was a little over two decades between them, there was little difference in their appearances aside from the streak of grey striped boldly against Celia's temple, a manifestation of years of hard work with very little dance involved.

Cherish had always excelled more at academics than dance, though. Throughout her schooling, she could feel her mother's loneliness and fought to keep her connection with her as best she could. She made time to visit her each summer throughout college, returning a little taller and wiser each time she knocked on Celia's door. Aside from the few times she was ill or immersed in her studies, Cherish always made an effort to return home. Her heart-shaped face beamed with eager satisfaction when she showed up on Celia's doorstep with good news or looked drawn and sullen when she retreated there after her heart had been broken.

On a few occasions after she'd begun her first year of college, Cherish had come back to find that Celia also had times when things clearly hadn't worked out the way she planned. Cherish could easily recall the few times she held back surprise as the door swung open on a scene she barely recognized—her mother standing there with a hopeful smile and new love interest by her side. Celia had been alone for many years, after all. Tyron, in his teens at that point, was old enough to accept his mother's needs. So, Cherish had been polite to the four men she'd met in as many years and joined Tyron in comforting their mother whenever she returned to find her alone again.

But this visit, Cherish had returned to stay with her mother because she'd been the one who'd needed comforting. Things with her boyfriend hadn't been going well, and their last fight had left her so shaken that she'd fled to her mother's place for solace only to find Celia with Darren, a man who made her feel uneasy at best.

In her twenty-two years of life, Cherish had never laid eyes on someone she'd instantly disliked more than Darren. But instead of heading home, she'd felt compelled to stay and make sure her mother wasn't being taken advantage of by this new man. Her mother wasn't wealthy by any means, but she kept a comfortable home and tended to fall for those she deemed in need of nurturing.

So, Cherish stayed and observed her mother's companion closely. She'd even asked her brother Tyron about him whenever she could, though he had little interaction with the man.

"He's alright, I guess. He gets weird when he gets his headaches, though. A little irritated. That's when I stay out of his way," Tyron said dismissively before putting his headphones back in his ears.

Cherish couldn't help but smile at her little brother's strange habit of watching television while listening to music in his headphones. As she walked toward Tyron's door, she reached to turn his TV off on her way out but paused to hear what sounded like an interesting broadcast.

"If you're just now joining us, we want to recap the strange report we received from several U.S. naval officers who claim that they have been unable to submerge since yesterday," the newscaster reported in a bland voice. The scene cut away to a man in uniform.

"It's as if our subs are being pulled right out of the water. Everything we checked was working okay…we really don't know how this is happening," the naval officer said authoritatively. Cherish pressed the button on the side of Tyron's TV and left the room.

At nineteen, Tyron stood well over six feet and didn't spend much time outside his room except when he was headed to the kitchen for food or off to school or work. Tyron had become withdrawn after losing his basketball scholarship to a knee injury that left him in a wheelchair for several months and a pin in his knee for the rest of his life. Though he'd regained his ability to walk and was able to attend a local university, both Celia and Cherish found it hard to console him. The Tyron they'd known always had a basketball under his arm since he could walk. And since Tyron's stories had all been about basketball, he'd discovered he had little else to say after the injury. He tried not to sulk in front of his mother, but that effort was as much about preserving his pride as it was about avoiding her sympathy. So, he forced his interactions as much as he could, but on the days his knee caused him more pain than usual, he said almost nothing at all.

And on those days, Cherish had to remain vigilant enough for the both of them.

Cherish had witnessed the way Darren had already crawled into her mother's head like a black magic spell, regaling her with war stories about the metal plate in his skull and smiling at her in a way that had rendered Celia all but powerless. But with Cherish, Darren wasn't as talkative. More than a few times, there had been awkward silences between them as they passed each other in the kitchen, but Darren only managed a gruff sounding 'Good morning' or a 'Hey' as he poured his coffee and retired to Celia's room or the living room.

Aside from their stilted interactions, Darren's evening ritual of chasing his pain medication with several drinks each evening was also unsettling for Cherish, but Celia had quietly reminded her that he'd been badly injured in the war and that sometimes the plate in his skull gave him such pain that drinking was just his way of soothing it.

"Who are we to judge? We have no idea how it feels to go to war or have a thing like that in our heads," Celia had defended Darren fiercely. Afterward, Cherish softened her demeanor toward him as best she could.

After her second night there, Cherish remembered her mother's words and decided to join him in the living room as he drank beer and awaited her mother's return from work. Cherish had learned that the metal plate in Darren's head had enabled him to claim that he was disabled on paper even though he was able-bodied enough for most tasks, so he collected his checks and spent his days fixing things around her mother's house or running errands. He never stayed out long, and after Cherish had become accustomed to his quiet ways, she decided that she should at least give him a chance for her mother. He was handsome enough, tall, square-jawed, and meticulously groomed like her father had been. The only time he even appeared mildly undone was after he'd taken the pain medication for his head.

Now, as Cherish stood in the cool darkness of her closet, she wondered how she'd missed something so dark in the man.

How'd Tyron miss it too? Cherish thought hopelessly, tears welling in her eyes at the thought of Tyron.

Even though Cherish had been there for less than a week, she did notice that Darren's behavior had gone from quiet and agreeable when her mother was present to stand-offish when she wasn't. But today, with her brother and mother's whereabouts unaccounted for, there'd been an even bigger departure from his regular behavior. She noticed that he hadn't taken medication for his head. Instead, he'd spent most of the evening alternating between drinking cognac and beer. Upon seeing this, Cherish had decided to avoid him all evening after she returned from her day of visiting with friends. She's heard about several accidents on the road that day anyway due to a strange electrical storm, so coming home seemed the safest idea.

Concerned with Darren's behavior, she'd repeatedly called her mother and inquired about when she and her brother would be home but got no answer. Meanwhile, Darren sat on their old burgundy sofa in his sweatpants, with empty bottles accumulating on their coffee table as the hours rolled by.

After most of the evening had been uneventful, Cherish had decided to brave the living room twice. First, she'd gone to get food from the kitchen, and a second time to get her cell phone. Each time Darren had watched her in a way she didn't care for, but she forced presumptuous thoughts out of her head and feigned warmth.

"Have you heard from Ma? I heard a storm is rolling through here, and she might need to get picked up," Cherish asked over her shoulder as she headed back to her room after retrieving her phone.

"She says it's bad out there. It's not raining, but people been gettin' into accidents. She said she has a ride already, but it'll take them hours with the freeway the way it is," Darren's eyes had become narrow slits from all the alcohol he'd consumed, and since he frowned as he spoke, the crease between his pronounced brows made his whole face appear more menacing than it had earlier.

"Well, did you eat? Are you ok?" Cherish found that she could not maintain eye contact with Darren as she spoke.

"I'm alright. Just trying to figure out a way to pass the time," Darren leaned forward and placed the bottle of beer he was sipping on the coffee table in front of him. Then he stood up.

"You wanna catch the news out here?" Darren smiled wryly and motioned for her to sit. There was a swollen, purplish bruise on the top of his left hand she hadn't noticed before, though it stood out against the tawny beige color of his skin.

"How's your head?" Cherish asked, changing the subject.

"It's alright tonight. Decided to lay off those meds for once, though. They really knock me out. Think I'd rather stay up tonight. Catch some football, maybe," Darren saw her peek at his hand and jammed it into his pocket. He ran the other hand across the silver-tinged waves atop his head before returning to his seat.

"Oh. Ok. I'm going to grab some leftovers and catch up on some reading until Ma gets home— "Cherish began, but Darren had interrupted her.

"You really look like her," said Darren. He'd cocked his head to the side and let his eyes crawl over Cherish's tall, slender frame as he spoke.

Cherish crumpled her face at the intrusion, but Darren appeared unbothered.

"Lean and brown. How tall are you?" Darren raised an eyebrow at Cherish, who now stood, mouth agape, with her eyes flitting between Darren and the door.

"E-excuse me. I have to check something," Cherish said and walked briskly toward the front door.

"I wouldn't go out there right now," Darren said calmly, but he didn't get up to follow her.

Cherish had ignored him, anyway. She'd already turned the handle and headed down the hallway to the front door of the apartment building. At that moment, she wished she'd remembered her car keys.

At least she had her phone with her. She opened the door and stepped out onto the landing that led to the parking lot before she froze. She blinked once, rubbed her eyes, and looked once more at the scene around her. Some of the signs around the perimeter of the parking lot outside were vibrating.

Even stranger, several cars were blocking the only entrance out of the lot, all abandoned and facing every direction. Cherish could see that some of the driver's side doors were open.

Gerald, an old man who'd lived in her mother's building for years, called down from his balcony.

"Been like that all evening," Gerald said, rather amused. His eyes twinkled in his creased face as he continued. "And look over there," he said, pointing at the sky.

Cherish squinted at what she saw. There was an array of colors in the sky. The colors swirled at an inconsistent speed, alternating colors with either dizzying speed or with a slow, gentle rhythm. Cherish stood mesmerized.

"Whatever it is, I'm ready. But you best go back inside, young lady." At this, Gerald plucked at one of his suspenders with his right thumb in a merry gesture. Cherish raised an eyebrow and realized she'd never seen Gerald dressed in such a way unless he was headed for church. His white hair was matted with pomade and slicked back. He wore Oxfords, a starched white shirt beneath a dark blazer, and matching trousers. He held a hat in his left hand, too.

As Cherish digested Gerald's words and manner of dress, she was bathed in a sick feeling.

I've never known him to go to church, thought Cherish. *He looks as if he's dressed to die. This is what he wants to be buried in.*

Cherish could feel her hands trembling. Fortunately, her

panicked thoughts were interrupted by a voice coming through the old radio on Gerald's balcony.

"We are being told that our towers are …best stay inside your homes…objects made of metal…all at this time…." the broadcaster's message was broken with static, but Cherish gathered that it was best for her to go back inside. She'd only come out to see if her reception would be better, and she quickly discerned that t wasn't. As Cherish turned to walk back into the building, she swore she saw a yield sign wriggle loose from the ground and zip upward into the sky.

When Cherish came back into the apartment, she found that Darren had moved from his place on the sofa.

Maybe he left, Cherish thought hopefully as she headed down the hallway to her bedroom. When she did, she saw Darren exiting her brother's room.

"Hey," Darren said sheepishly. This time, it was he who was unable to meet Cherish's gaze. "Just borrowing some gauze from your brother's room. I figured he keeps stuff for his basketball injury in there."

"There's gauze in the medicine cabinet in the bathroom," Cherish had taken care to sound cold.

"Oh yeah," Darren said. Cherish thought he sounded far less apologetic as he continued. "Well, I guess I'm just turned around because I have a lot on my mind tonight. Forgot to check in there. I'll check now, though. Need some muscle rub anyway. Mashed up my hand pretty bad today working on some stuff for Celia."

Cherish had eyed him suspiciously and continued toward her bedroom, with thoughts of Gerald's words on replay in her mind.

'I'm ready,' Cherish heard Gerald's words echo in her thoughts throughout the night.

But now, as Cherish's eyes fully adjusted to the darkness inside her bedroom closet, she had the same thought that she'd had after hearing Darren's excuse for leaving her brother's room. And it was the same feeling she'd had each time she caught him staring at her inappropriately all evening.

I missed something, Cherish thought, more frustrated than she'd ever been.

Hearing him mention my mother caught me off guard, Cherish thought as she shifted her weight off her sore ankle.

What a manipulative son of a bitch. I could've stopped it, Cherish bit her lip at the thought.

She tried once more to focus on the door of her bedroom but thinking about what had gone wrong that night allowed her mind to shift focus from the pain, so she continued to think about what had transpired. Methodically, her brain recounted the moment Darren had revealed himself for who she'd suspected him of being all along. Cherish decided to focus on that moment because she knew that focusing on what Darren had done to her brother would keep her from collapsing. Her anger would help her stand upright, despite the pain.

So, she forced her mind through it again, pulling herself away from the pain in her ankle until the medication she'd taken started to kick in.

After her awkward exchange with Darren earlier, Cherish had rushed back to the safety of her room and shut the door to make the call she desperately needed to make to her mother. Only, her phone hadn't worked. She'd cursed as quietly as she could while trying her mother's number over and over. An error recording had played each time. Cherish cracked her door. Even though she had no phone service in the strange storm, she had been relieved to hear the sound of Darren's loud snoring wafting from the living room. The snorts and other unpleasant sounds his body belted out as he slept offered Cherish some comfort. Finally, Darren had returned to the routine she'd observed from the last few days…and Cherish loved all manner of routines. She calmed herself by reasoning that their earlier exchange had been a misunderstanding.

This night is just different because my mother isn't here to stop his drinking and tuck him in, Cherish nodded to herself. *He's disoriented from not taking his pain meds, and he's acting weird tonight, but there's no need to bother my mother right now. She's had it hard enough.*

She'd crept down the hallway and allowed herself a short

but soothingly hot shower before tiptoeing back to her room. Darren, who appeared to be sleeping soundly, didn't budge as she'd crept by once more in a towel with her clothes clutched to her frame.

After returning from her shower, Cherish had turned on her TV to hear more news about what was going on outside and tried once more to relax. As she gathered her pajamas from her drawer, she moved slowly, distracted by thoughts of her mother.

Should I tell her? Cherish's stomach had churned violently at the thought.

A loud thump broke Cherish's inner ramblings. The thump came from the living room and was followed by a slew of curse words. Darren had awakened early and was stumbling around her mother's living room, checking each bottle and can that he could find.

Then, he had been at her door. First, Cherish thought he was turned around, still disoriented. Then she realized he was just standing there, staring. He said nothing.

"You sack of shit. What do you think you're doing?" Cherish had uttered the words without even thinking.

"Just saying 'hello' Cherry," Darren said, and Cherish was at first unsure if he'd mispronounced her name by accident because he was still intoxicated or done it as a sexual advance. "Shit. You been acting weird all day."

She paused for a moment, searching his face as she moved to close her bedroom door.

His breath had been rancid from his evening diet of beer, cognac, and corn chips, and before Cherish could calculate whether his words were indeed sinister, she began to see that he was bulging through the thin sweats he wore. Seeing the shock and disgust on her face seemed to amuse Darren. He chuckled as he moved back a few steps, allowing Cherish to close the door. Her heart pounded as she heard his footsteps move toward the bathroom. Then, her mind had turned to thoughts of Tyron.

She allowed a horrific thought to enter her mind and nestle itself there. It galloped deeper inside her mind's eye, riding on the back of Darren's sinister chuckle, which had already slithered into her thoughts once again.

He's done something to Tyron, Cherish thought it and then immediately knew it to be true.

Too encompassed with fear to clothe herself fully, she peered outside her bedroom to see the blade of light spilling from under the bathroom door. Then she crept to Tyron's room.

Inside the room, Cherish moved quickly and quietly in the dark. The room smelled foul, but that wasn't necessarily unusual for her teenage brother's room. He'd toss his clothes all over his room after basketball practice and had never been concerned about neatness. Even though nothing appeared out of the ordinary to Cherish, she was drawn to his closet. Her mind on autopilot, she rifled through the piles of clothes on the floor before she lifted something weightier than the rest of the soiled socks and gym clothes she'd been scooping in her arms. She lifted what she knew to be Tyron's limb, wrapped in something. She felt further. It was a sheet. Cherish took a long shaky breath with her eyes squeezed shut. When she opened them, she found that her eyes had adjusted to the blue-toned shadows of her brother's closet.

Still, Cherish would not turn toward his body. She'd instead listened carefully for sounds of a toilet flushing or water running; she'd listened for Darren. As she did, she'd allowed her fingers to feel up the length of Tyron's body, which had been placed in a seated position, his knees bowed awkwardly upward due to his height. His body had been shrouded, but his face hadn't. Cherish could feel the cold blood congealed on the corner of his bottom lip. Her hands shook with rage as she snatched her fingers away. She'd hugged her knees to her chest for a brief moment before she'd remembered her time limit. Then, Cherish moved toward his door with a fluidity her body hadn't known before that very moment. As she poked her head out and angled it toward the bathroom with her body still inside Tyron's room, Cherish had been relieved to see that light still spilled from under the door, and she tiptoed noiselessly down the hallway toward the end table where her car keys were.

Only, they weren't there.

Did I move them? Cherish didn't allow herself to circle back in her memory to try to recall where she'd left them because she sensed there wasn't enough time, so she'd ventured toward the kitchen instead.

Her mother's old, wooden knife rack was in plain view near the sink because she'd left the stove light on earlier when she'd warmed her food. The dim light it cast was just enough to for her to discern the largest knife and lift it from the rack.

Gently, Cherish said to herself, sliding the knife upward.

"ARGHHhHHhh! MY FUCKING HEAD! NONE OF THIS SHIT WORKS!" Darren screamed in the bathroom. Cherish stood petrified with her hand on the knife handle, listening. Her heart raced furiously as she heard what must've been pill bottles hitting the floor of the bathroom.

Run! Cherish's inner self shrieked in frustration, willing her limbs out of atrophy. But it was too late. Cherish had heard the door to the bathroom burst open, and because Darren was now closer to the apartment's only exit besides the windows of the bedrooms, she'd grabbed the knife and bolted back toward her bedroom.

As she did, she'd seen Darren stagger out of the bathroom. He'd held one hand to his temple and felt along the wall as he did.

"CHERISH! I'm not gonna lie, I've had a long day, baby," Darren had sobbed and laughed as he began his one-sided conversation with Cherish. "All day, I've felt just like something's been pullin' the plate right out of my skull since this afternoon. Made my temper a little short, you know? PTSD's what they call it. I didn't mean to hurt your brother— he just caught me in a bad mood. And…I'm not going to hurt you or Celia. But I do need you to help me feel better, okay?"

Cherish, who'd been standing at the threshold to her bedroom listening intently, positioned herself to run toward the front door again. But when she did, Darren produced a revolver from the small of his back.

"Now there. Calm down a little and hear me out." Darren said to Cherish. He'd caught her by her waist as she'd tried to run and effortlessly flung her against the hallway wall, mangling her ankle in the process.

She had lain there for a full minute, giving Darren time to grab his half-drunken glass of cognac from the kitchen. He drank it in one gulp and stretched noisily with the revolver still in his hand, raising his arms high above his head. From where she sat on the ground and where he stood in the kitchen, he'd looked like an immovable giant to Cherish in that moment. So, she'd done the only thing she hadn't allowed herself to do up until that point. She cried.

Then, she screamed and cried.

"You killed Tyron! For...what?! Why?!" Cherish barely managed the words as she tried to pull herself up using the doorknob to her room but slid helplessly back down, shocked by the crippling pain in her ankle. She knew then that she couldn't run, as each movement sent red-hot pain coursing through her left side from her ankle.

"I'm a man who did a lot for other people all his damn life; that's why!" Darren roared. "And what I get out this shit?! Huh? HUH?! A fuckin' metal plate in my head? To take care of some old lady with a moody son that aint even mine?"

Darren threw his head back and laughed at that point, sending chills through Cherish that momentarily warred with the pain pulsating in her ankle.

"And now they mean to tell me the whole world is gone to shit outside, and we all might die tonight without me ever gettin' SHIT I WANTED?! No. That aint how this works, baby," Darren ran a hand over his hair and placed the glass and gun on the counter.

"That's not our fault! If you didn't want to be with my mother, why are you here? And she's coming BACK! It's just a storm—" Cherish started, but Darren cut her tearful admonishment short by abruptly sweeping the glass off the counter, enraged. As it shattered into a million pieces, Cherish had again looked longingly at the door.

"It aint no regular storm, dammit!" Darren screamed. His

face flushed crimson red, and a large vein along his temple grew more visible as he continued. "I been around the world and aint seen nothing like this! If you hadn't been struttin' around all night you would've seen that it *aint* NO REGULAR STORM. Tell you what, though. If I gotta die tonight I'ma do *exactly* what I wanna before I do," Darren had finished his rant calmly and picked up the revolver from the kitchen counter once more.

But then he'd just stood there, red-faced, with his chest heaving—despite seeing that Cherish had stood up and was facing him, carefully balancing on her good foot and holding onto the doorknob of her bedroom for leverage. Cherish had thrown him a steely glare, but he seemed unfazed.

Darren returned the weapon to the small of his back, ran his fingers through his hair again, and collected a clean glass and from the dishrack. Then he withdrew a half-empty bottle of cognac from one of the cabinets. After poured the fresh drink, he continued.

"Phwew!" Darren said as he leaned on the counter. "I saw you in a few pictures before I met you. It was your mother who showed them to me," Darren took a sip of brown liquor, and his face formed a grimace that melted into a half-smile in a manner of seconds. "You know, this does more for my headaches than those pills ever could."

Darren chuckled, but Cherish had only stood there, still

as a gargoyle, listening.

"Anyway," Darren continued, "She told me you were coming to visit. And you know what? Even right then, I said to myself, 'Darren. You ole dawg…you be good, damn it.'"

Pain shot up Cherish's injured leg, and she hissed at its intensity. Then she pursed her lips shut and gritted her teeth to distract her from it as her eyes flitted around the apartment. Darren appeared not to notice and went on speaking, centering his gaze on the glass of cognac he held at eye level and not on Cherish.

"But tonight? I swear it's sum'n special 'bout it. It was sent for us. You walkin' around in that towel pretending like you ain't see me looking and askin' me if I was hungry. All that flirtin' let me know that what I was feelin' was alright. It was— it *is* natural," Darren had begun to slur his words.

"Fuck you." It was all Cherish had been able to manage as she limped into her bedroom. Darren laughed, and his laughter grew louder even after she'd closed her door. She'd wanted nothing more than to fling herself across her bed and collapse, but instead, she'd clicked on her light and quickly rummaged through her bedroom door for pain pills. She hadn't dared to let go of the knife she'd grabbed from the kitchen, so she gripped it in her left hand as she balanced herself against her dresser, leaning on her elbow as she used her right hand to rummage through her top drawer for anything to dull the pain. When she found the half-empty bottle, she swallowed four of the capsules hurriedly, unsure if Darren was walking toward her bedroom door.

But he hadn't been. Cherish realized that as she listened to his intoxicated rambling. She hurriedly bound her ankle with a slouch sock, then turned on the television to see if what Darren had said earlier was true.

"Mmmmm…fired up tonight, baby!" Darren yelled drunkenly from the kitchen.

Cherish glanced at her window but knew in her heart she couldn't make the climb down. She tried to calm herself instead. She took several deep breaths and willed the medication she'd taken earlier to cycle through her bloodstream and swirl her pain away into a dull, hollow thump instead of the piercing shriek it was at the moment.

In the meantime, I'm gonna fight like hell, Cherish thought as hot tears streamed down her face. *If he did what he did to Tyron, it's no telling what he'll do to mama when she gets back. If she gets back…*

She clicked on her television and headed for her closet, as it was the furthest point from the door. Cherish struggled to quiet her sobs and hoped the television would mask the sound until she got her bearings. She could feel the pain in her leg begin to lessen a bit as she concentrated on the voices that drifted from the TV.

As she stood in the closet, the smell of old familiar things and the sound of the newscast soothed her a little, but her mind still played the events of the night over and over, each time more rapidly.

The way Tyron's blood felt against her fingers.

The cool plastic of the knife in her left hand.

She nodded her head slowly as she processed those thoughts, weighing them as she concentrated on her escape. Finding no other distraction, she focused on the newscaster's voice even harder.

"Reports of this peculiar event are now coming in from across the globe. Something appears to be affecting metal objects—" the broadcast was cut short just as it had begun, and the TV abruptly went dark.

But Cherish had already absorbed each word the newscaster spoke, and as the pain in her ankle faded into the background of her thoughts, she began to focus keenly on her surroundings. Even when the lights suddenly went out in a flash that would've startled her even on a regular night, Cherish found that she had calmed herself so much that she didn't flinch. She breathed in the moldy, familiar smells of her closet. She reached into the darkness around her, grabbed the first thing she could find, and covered her abdomen, which was icy to the touch at this point since she'd only put on a bra and sweats before the whole ordeal. She slipped the old tee-shirt over her head as she heard Darren's footsteps approaching her door

"*Whatever it is, I'm ready,*" is what Cherish had heard Mr. Gerald say earlier on his balcony.

And I am too, Cherish thought as she felt the medication do its work. She gripped the knife with clammy hands.

"Phwew! Lights out! This night was meant for us, Cherish!" Darren yelled excitedly. Then, he kicked her bedroom door easily off its hinges and fell forward onto the carpet in a drunken stupor. But he didn't stay floored for long.

After looking around for a moment, Darren pushed himself up on his elbows and crouched on all fours to look under Cherish's bed. When he did, Cherish limped to his side and, seizing the only moment when he was at a bigger disadvantage than she was, stabbed him in his back as hard as she could.

Darren swung his left arm backward, grabbing for the hilt of the blade. A red spot flowered around the blade's handle and spread quickly as Darren bled profusely.

"BITCH!" Darren sputtered. "You little BITCH!" But Cherish was already limping toward the door. Darren, powered by rage and adrenaline and numb from alcohol and pain medication, quickly recovered and pulled the blade out of his shoulder with a grunt. Then, he swiped at Cherish's good ankle.

Already off-balance from her bad ankle, Cherish slipped as she dodged the swing of the perforated blade. The maneuver saved her good ankle from being slashed but left her face down on the floor. Instantly, Darren scrambled for her, grabbed the waist of her pajama pants, and snatched them off with one hand.

"No!" Cherish thrashed her good leg backward and tried to kick Darren in the face as hard as she could. She landed a few kicks before she felt the barrel of the revolver against the back of her head. She could hear his low, sinister laughter as he wriggled the gun through her braids and pressed it against her scalp. Cherish could feel the coolness of the barrel just as she felt the warmth of Darren's breath against her ear.

"All this fuss to ruin a night the universe put together for us? A night alone with just us two?" Darren slurred his whispers, and his breath was laden with alcohol.

He undid his trousers with one hand and continued to hold the gun against the back of Cherish's head with the other. Pinned to the ground, Cherish sobbed loudly from the pain as she bore the full weight of Darren's frame. Her ribs pressed into the floor, and she could barely breathe. She squeezed her eyes shut in defeat as she felt Darren position himself to enter her from behind.

The room swirled, and Cherish began losing air as Darren thrust in the dark. Disoriented, he only succeeded in grinding against her. He lifted himself to find her again, snatching her hips upwards with one hand and forcing her legs further apart by spreading his own knees. As he did, he bumped her bad leg. The pain renewed itself once more and was so intense Cherish was sure she'd begun to hallucinate.

She first imagined that she could no longer feel the cool barrel of the gun against her scalp. Then she felt that Darren had become weightless somehow. Whatever the case, her pain lessened, and she could breathe again, so she decided to open her eyes. When she did, she saw that the walls were bathed in pink.

I'm dying, thought Cherish. *And all these colors must be part of my transition. Maybe I'm halfway through a doorway, and everything is distorted as I pass through.*

Just as she was beginning to accept her thoughts, her concentration was broken by Darren's hands grabbing ahold of her hips, pulling her up and toward him once more. Resigned, Cherish let her full weight collapse into the floor without trying to fight him. She rested one cheek against the carpet, awaiting her fate. The only thing she let herself be fully aware of was that the walls had changed from pink to green.

Then purple.

Then orange-y purple with blotches of green.

God sent me a rainbow, Cherish thought calmly. *Glad tidings from Tyron as I die.*

Faintly, she could feel something dripping on the back of her tee-shirt. It was wet. The light coming through her window flashed brilliantly now. Swirling and blending and bursting.

Splat! Drip! Splat!

She imagined it was paint from the colors as they swirled, splattering her back and buttocks. Cherish could feel its warmth as each droplet landed and made its slow, rolling path along her sides. Then, she heard a rattling sound to her left.

No! Cherish thought stubbornly, tears pooling onto the carpet beneath her cheek. She fought to find the serenity she felt just moments before while watching the colors swirl. *I'm dying, and I'm ready. If you're listening up there, let me be.*

Cherish could see Tyron's face and her mother's too, but the rattling near her left ear grew louder and more distracting. Finally, she turned her head just in time to see the bloody knife, which had been lying just a few feet from her on the carpet, whip itself into the air.

Cherish pulled herself onto her elbows now. The pain had lessened because of the pills she'd taken, but her ankle still throbbed. She carefully pulled herself into a cross-legged seated position on the carpet and touched a hand to her back. She looked left and right but saw no sign of Darren. The whole room began to shake and rattle. Bracelets zipped off of her wrists and into the air. A spoon from a cereal bowl on her nightstand also jetted up into the air.

Cherish finally looked at her fingers, which were covered in blood. The small pendant necklace she wore tugged itself away from her neck, popping its clasp as it zipped into the air. Cherish allowed her eyes to follow it, sharp memories cutting through the fog in her brain as she did.

The hydrant. The sign. METAL OBJECTS, Cherish quickly angled her neck toward the ceiling of her bedroom and saw Darren.

He appeared to be awkwardly pasted up to the ceiling. The bottom of his torso and his legs hung limply, and his left arm dangled. But the right hand that held the gun had glued his entire right arm to the ceiling.

Darren's eyes bulged while his whole face hemorrhaged blood. His mouth was stuck in an 'O' formation, and his head and right hand trembled as the strange force held him captive.

Metal objects, Cherish rocked back and forth as Darren's blood rained down on her, splattering her hair and face. *Metal OBJECTS. METAL OBJECTS.*

"Metal...," Cherish said quietly to herself as the details of the strange storm shifted into place in her tired mind. "Metal plate...in his skull."

Cherish would've sat in shock forever had a familiar voice not beckoned her from the doorway.

"Cherish...WATCH OUT!" Celia stood in the doorway, covered in dust and blood. Her earlobes were bleeding, but her gait was steady as she moved to lock her arms under her daughter's and pull her into the hallway. Just as she did, Celia and Cherish heard a gurgling, sucking sound before Darren's limp body fell to the ground with a large, bloody hole in the back of his head surrounded by shards of his skull and grey bits of his brain.

Neither Celia nor Cherish could speak. They just held onto each other tightly in the darkness of the hallway, rocking gently back and forth. Hours passed this way as they sat in a trance, watching the colors continue to dance and swirl against the walls. There they stayed, holding each other tightly and silently until the small window at the end of the dark corridor allowed the sun to reach in and swallow the colors that danced gleefully with the shadows on the wall. Once the sun was up in full force, Celia helped Cherish to the window, and they looked out to see that the storm had finally passed.

The Predictor

Telkor organized all the things in his modestly sized pod and recorded a holoprojection for Porma, whom he'd persuaded to visit the market in anticipation of his meeting, and possible detainment. He knew that she could return soon if his plans for her were somehow interrupted, but he also figured he'd be gone if she did, so it wouldn't matter. Inspector Preedo was already on his way from Tower Nine, and theirs was a known rivalry, no matter the professional etiquette they kept with each other.

He could see a hint of his reflection in the circular window near his pod entrance. He blinked one eye at a time, as he often did when flustered, and gazed out at the domes close to the ground, chiefly reserved for the poorest in Vaxxor, then upward to the glass obelisks and curvilinear towers reserved for the wealthy and otherwise elite. His was a planet full of refined, peaceful beings, originally settled by a group of ambitious explorers who shared a common goal: the freedom to engage in eugenics and rapid gestation, two endeavors that had been outlawed on their previous planet. After a few dozen millennia, one could look upon the modern-day Vaxxorians and see which features they'd abandoned in favor of others and how those who bore the resulting phenotypes fared.

There were those who walked upright, having spliced with Earthian humanoids and those whose ancestors had chosen to incorporate genes from non-avian reptilian species sourced from several planets to maintain the fluidity and speed of four-legged movement. Telkor observed that many of the latter resembled the Dinosauria of old Earth that lived long before the planet's biome became uninhabitable for most of its species.

Telkor's mind swirled with the gravity of it; Vaxxor had observed that the end was near for the aquatic planet and, in somewhat of a panic, ordered Telkor to oversee their last extraction. Six female specimens, all plucked from the midst of escalating temperature spikes, rising sea levels, and impending worldwide famine, and all but one had perished on the journey home to Vaxxor.

And now, Telkor nodded pensively to himself, *there is but one specimen left.*

When he was first appointed, Telkor thoroughly enjoyed the privilege of being the sole Predictor in his district. It was a hard-won, stressful job, but he had always been wholly suited for it. Now, Preedo was sure that he was suited for the job too.

Worse, Telkow was sure that no matter the outcome of the day, there was no chance that it would end with him retaining his position as Predictor.

Curse you, Preedo, Telkor seethed as he adjusted the collar of his full-length uniform coat.

One of the planet's suns was setting, and the colors it cast wrapped the densely populated district and all its towering structures in a glittering sheen that looked nearly iridescent. Telkor continued to wait by the window, patiently watching Vaxxorians traverse the enclosed bridgeways that connected the upper structures and those who swarmed along the pathways below. Watching them, he considered that if he was found guilty of the offense that Preedo accused him of—the abduction of Earthian C6—and somehow managed to get pardoned from the sentence it carried—death by public incineration—he'd certainly be relegated to the lesser punishment of exile to an area that the elite in his society called 'The Lowly Domes.' Worst of all, as Predictor, he was keenly aware that either outcome was likely.

"But we *will* see, won't we?" Telkor murmured to himself.

He heard the tube platform stop just outside his door, signaling Preedo's arrival. He briskly walked over and rolled both eyes in the direction of the scanner to unlock it. Because the door slid upward and open before Preedo could knock, the tall figure stood hunkered in the doorway with his scaly hand poised to do so for a moment before lowering it to his side.

"You came alone?" Telkor was genuinely surprised. "Come in, then. Welcome. Porma is out at the moment."

Preedo ducked and angled his large body to cross the threshold into Telkor's tidy pod, his tail swishing behind his massive frame. The doorway was a little over eight feet tall, and Telkor's elongated head and lanky body passed through it with only a few inches to spare. For Preedo, who preferred to stand upright unless he had to move particularly fast, even eight feet was a few inches shy of his full height.

"I see," Preedo huffed his words out, visibly annoyed by his awkward entry. "And yes, I'm alone. You needn't worry yourself…yet. The data is intact; I am simply here to query you about your recommendation and hear your thoughts on the disappearance of C6."

"Of course," Telkor motioned for Preedo to sit, sweeping his slender, olive-green hands toward the sitting area, an arrangement of cubical structures that protruded from the floor of the pod. "I'm quite prepared to explain myself."

"Very well, then, Preedo touched a device strapped to his girthy wrist, and a light turned on, casting an orange glow on his squamous skin. "I'm required to inform you that this interview is being recorded and to formally state what it concerns. Do you understand?"

Telkor nodded. He was already bored and struggled to

keep one eye from peering toward his kitchen.

I should have eaten before this ordeal.

"You know the history of our society and why we chose to retain parthenogenesis as our main method of reproducing," Preedo paused, and Telkor realized that he was waiting for an answer, so he nodded again, and Preedo continued. "We are not particularly sentimental beings, and neither were our ancestors."

"Indeed," Telkor stared at him listlessly, already sure of the direction of the interrogation and utterly disappointed by Preedo's lack of brevity.

"So, you do understand why cataloging species which are less advanced is of use to us," Preedo said the last part slowly as if addressing an individual with a head injury or a childling. "It helps us stay abreast of threats and uphold our sampling and breeding program. This quells the need for violent conquests and acquisitions—you know this."

Telkor said nothing. He stared at him intently and offered another brief nod.

"Your role as Predictor is to render data from this program so that our rapid gestations go to plan," Preedo gestured emphatically as he spoke, and Telkor fought the urge to stare at his talons as he did, which were far more treacherous than the almost humanoid nails on his own forelimbs. "It's why I don't understand your sudden interest in this particular primate. The nearly hairless duopeds of that planet—all of their physiology is largely the same, and we've been splicing with them for many years. Yet, in your report, you write that the findings from C6's reflect that she is not a worthy candidate, despite being no different than the others. Did you not?"

"Yes, I did," Telkor leaned forward and drummed his nails on the cube between them, then answered. "I wrote what I wrote for several reasons, and none of them are sentimental. But I assume you alluded to me being sentimental because my species is anatomically similar to this specimen. So doesn't that make you a bit biased in this matter?"

Suddenly Preedo huffed, and an odd, high-pitched wheezing sound escaped from his horned nostrils. "I see that your tactic today is to deflect, but I'll ignore your insult for the moment, especially since I pride myself on being impartial to you despite our past differences. Let's move forward. You wrote: 'After reviewing the data from the specimen's projections, it is my opinion that we should terminate this program in favor of another, similar species.' No need for me to quote you exactly, but it's safe to say that you wrote other things that pointed to the fact that you came by this decision because of issues you discovered with its physiology. What did you mean by that?"

"Both our species, yours and mine, have organs that

function rather steadily," Telkor crossed his legs so that his ankle rested on his left knee, revealing the exoskeletal bottom of his right foot, and sighed. "This is because we've long since edited out any abnormalities that would affect us in the same manner as some primitive species. For instance, we have no fight-or-flight inclination, no strong urge to procreate at the onset of sexual maturity, and little—brazenness? That's the best way to put it. But most importantly, since we have successfully adapted asexual reproduction by fusing favorable amphibious and ceratopsian elements with our own genes, we have no need to look back nor breed upright invertebrates further. Truly, after what I've seen, I gauge that any more mixing could produce unstable, unpredictable offspring. My recommendation is for remote observation of their species only."

"Is that why you released C6?" Preedo scrunched his visage, and Telkor saw a flash of purple as he flicked his tongue from his rostrum.

"Have you not heard a word I said?" Telkor laughed incredulously and wriggled his evenly lengthy, webbed toes. "The thing is dangerous, even as part of an experimental breeding program."

"And you learned this how?" Preedo asked, flustered. "From what you ascertained from calculating its lifespan and heart rate? And a few dream projections? "

"Memory," Telkor corrected.

"A few memory projections, then?" Preedo scratched one of his two horns, and Telkor found it to be a repugnant sound.

Ugh, Telkor suppressed a grimace. *He always scratches his horn when he thinks. I'd prefer public incineration to that abhorrent sound on any given sun cycle.*

"Thousands, actually. Further, those projections were tied to instances that increased each specimen's heart rate, each quite different from the next. But I don't need to tell you what our Collector device does. We've been using it to qualify species for our program for nearly a millennia."

"Indeed, we have," Preedo's tone shifted from amiable to accusatory. "And in that time, do you know how many rejections we've had from Predictors like yourself? Three. Just…three."

"I stand by my recommendation and further contend that I have no knowledge of the whereabouts of C6," Telkor smoothed the fabric of his uniform cloak indignantly, his fingers brushing against its patches and insignias. "Vaxxor is a vast planet with a thriving trade market for illegal species in the Lower Dome communities; I suggest you start looking there. So, if there's nothing further, Porma will return shortly. I'm happy to continue this discussion in the headquarters. Tower Nine is but a few minutes away, and we could—"

"Why do you keep her as a companion here?" Preedo scratched the horn again, and the small space filled with the raspy sound of it. "Is she of use to you in some way?"

"Who? Porma?" Telkor lilted his voice pointedly.

"Never mind," Preedo didn't smile because his face was incapable of it, but Telkor heard the subtle swishing of his tail beneath his cloak, though Preedo had clearly taken pains to conceal it. "If you're going to continue this course of evasion, we can just move on."

He's pleased with something, and that can't be good, Telkor slouched deeper in his seat. *Ugh. Really should've eaten.*

"Just tell me this once more—what is it, specifically, that you observed in its projections?" Preedo pressed on, his voice tinged with curiosity.

"Many things," Telkor began, his tone calm and deliberate. "The specimen intentionally put itself in harm's way numerous times, which is significant considering that it is less than midway through its presumed lifespan (of 76-83 Earthian years). For instance, C6 routinely launched itself into the liquid that covers most of its planet, despite its respiratory system being unsuited for that task. Yet, it appeared to do so numerous times as part of what appears to be a collective ritual celebration of seasonal temperature fluctuations.

"Another disturbing finding is that it kept constant contact with its home-world's worst predator, which just happens to be its reproductive opposite, but...it maintained its close proximity for sexual gratification, not reproduction. I'm not exaggerating in the least, either. Earthian males have been the most violent adversaries to their female counterparts, subjugating, humiliating, and killing them for millennia, yet they are diametrically, pheromonally drawn to each other. Yet, they continue this contentious mingling even though they have other methods with which to reproduce offspring.

"I also found dozens of memories in the Collector's database in which C6 willingly drank poison while balancing itself on heightened walking apparatuses. In some of these memory projections, I observed her wearing another Earthian's head-fur on its head, like a closely fitting hat—on top of its own hair? Did I mention that one of its species' pastimes was to file into large viewing halls and watch projections that depicted its own kind being mutilated or killed—for enjoyment? Do you know what these instances all had in common, Preedo?"

"Well, it's here in the report if you'd give me just a moment to find it, but I'm sure you mean to tell me instead," Preedo suddenly stretched and yawned, and it sounded to Telkor like an ancient machine, contracting its squeaky, rusted parts.

"It's the *heart rate*, Preedo," Telkor said, uncrossing his legs and leaning forward. "In all of these random instances, C6 had a heart rate similar to the other Earthians we've tested. It was right there in the haptic read-outs for its projections. You know full well that our Collector is older than their era of intellectual enlightenment, Preedo, and I've studied the files from our first acquisitions there. What I truly believe is, the reason the latest scans are similar to the scans of their predecessors isn't because they're engaging in the same lifestyle—that would be impossible because they have no means to reproduce those conditions. So actually, therein lies the issue— the read-outs are similar because they've reached a point in their evolution in which they *long* for the dangers their ancestors faced."

"Are you saying that Earthians, having rid themselves of an existence of mere survival—one in which they battled harsh elements and warred with beasts several times their size—now miss it?" Preedo huff-scoffed then snorted.

"That is precisely what I'm saying," Telkor leaned back and crossed his arms again. "If you look at all the things they do for leisure, you'll find that most of it is a direct danger to them. Yet, the read-outs don't lie; dopamine and adrenaline levels, heart rates...they all point to those activities as the things their species enjoy the most, the things that exhilarate them. All the killing, barbaric means of sexual intercourse, and proximity to danger—in other words, all the things their predecessors once did to sustain the continuation of their species—they now engage in for fun. So, under their veil of order and self-control, they really are as chaotic as they are bored, Preedo, and as Predictor, I have long observed that the combination of those two traits makes a species dangerous. It is my summation that we should not intermingle with them any further than we already have. Look at their planet? All their thrill-seeking has caused them to nearly self-eradicate. We should abandon course and look for other, similar species to glean."

Porma is five minutes late. She's rarely late. This must mean...

"Ahh, I see you've deduced that Porma hasn't arrived," Preedo said gingerly, and Telkor could see his tail swishing out of the corner of his right eye. "So rude of me. I let you prattle on with this diversion when I should've taken a moment to mention that she isn't coming."

Telkor said nothing, even though he innately knew that Preedo regarded his silence as fear. As he continued speaking, Preedo's mouth was slightly open, revealing two rows of sharp, uniform teeth. Telkor realized that it was the closest thing to a smile Preedo could manage.

"I must also apologize for misleading you about something earlier," Preedo oozed his words out in a faux-remorseful tone. "I think I avoided admitting it because I'm in your home, and it seemed ungracious of me to say. But...*you were right* when you said I was biased, Telkor."

He rose to his feet and began to pace, his tail swishing behind him. When he reached the pod's window, he stopped and continued with his back to Telkor.

"In fact, I'd wager that the uppers from Tower Nine sent me here precisely for that reason. You see, they happen to know that I don't like you. But not just you; I don't like *your type*. The long heads. The pompously upright, primate-humanoid bodies and uselessly long fingers sicken me. Further, I think your anatomical proximity to the Earthian specimen C6 does *indeed* dilute your judgment and render you sympathetic, which is why you simply cannot be trusted to be forthright in this instance."

Look at him, Telkor thought as he fought the urge to glare at Preedo. *His beady eyes are practically glowing with self-satisfaction. I suppose I'll pivot to my secondary plan in a moment, depending upon how his next few questions go.*

Telkor grit his triangular teeth for a moment, then spoke, "Is there anything else you'd like to add to that insult? Perhaps a swift kick to my abdomen? And it's *you* who I can't trust to be unbiased. You've been after my job for over a hundred sun cycles. Am I supposed to believe you aren't elated to raise this charge against me? Knowing full well you're next in line to replace me if I fall?"

"You like doing that, don't you?" Preedo hissed. "All of the sarcasm and condescending that you do? Well, you may not understand my ancestors' choice for gene modification, and I may not understand yours, but clearly, there were some traits that mine found favorable to yours. Yours valued the lengthy bodies, bipedal movement, and lack of tails, and mine chose other groupings of features that yours likely overlooked as inferior. But I *like* what I am...and *who* I am, Telkor."

"As do I," Telkor calculated that Preedo had approximately two minutes to detain him before the default outcome commenced.

So, he stalled.

"And for the record," Telkor continued pontifically, "I don't dislike your kind at all, and I'm hurt to hear that you've been harboring such feelings for me. Honestly, Preedo. If we give into such division, this planet will be thrown into chaos like those of the lesser ones we study. For instance, C6's cutaneous layer is a deeper color than some of our other specimens, and you would not *believe* some of the things I've encountered in the Collector database about that alone. Ghastly business, Preedo. It's beneath us."

"Perhaps," said Preedo with a toothy grin. "Well, then. How about this; how about we *celebrate* our differences instead? I'll celebrate how those amphibious eye sockets of yours lead you to believe that because you can see in two directions at once, you're always certain you know what's coming. And I'll celebrate that, while having a body type that you deem more cumbersome than yours, there is one thing that I thoroughly enjoy about it."

"Which is?" Telkor feigned curiosity.

"It's our sense of smell, Telkor," Preedo's grin withdrew, and he tapped a talon against his left nostril as he continued. "I'd rate it top five in this quadrant."

"Congratulations," Telkor replied, outwardly nonplussed.

Ahh yes, Telkor reasoned. *So it begins, as predicted. If I hadn't factored in his propensity to gloat, this may have gone differently, but Preedo always gloats.*

At this, Preedo shed his decorum, stood up abruptly, and roared, shaking with rage for several moments.

"I know the Earthian specimen is here!" Preedo screamed, then inhaled deeply as he let his eyes crawl over every inch of the Telkor's pod. "Her scent is strong here."

"And just how do you know that scent so well?" Telkor chuckled. "It seems you may have some explaining to do as well. Perhaps you have a little side-breeding program of your own?"

Preedo roared again, and it was a shattering sound that shook the entire space. Telkor could hear passersby exclaiming about the noise near his door, but he remained still.

"Calm down," Telkor continued. "You're creating a disturbance when really, all you're here to do is interrogate and leave, or interrogate me and take me in. Please make your decision so that we can both get on with our day."

"You'd let me cart you off to protect an Earthian?" The anger fell away from Preedo's face, and for a moment, he looked genuinely confused. "You know you'll be stripped of your role and likely exiled or killed—why do you persist in this? You said yourself that they are violent and unstable. Is one of them worth all of this trouble?"

"Absolutely not, which is precisely why I'm not hiding—" Telkor paused as his left eye registered movement in the corner. Then, he grinned.

"Fuck this," Camilla Gregory emerged from her hidden place in the sleeping quarters in the back of the pod, wearing a wetsuit with 00C6 across the chest, and brandishing a weapon nearly as long as her arm. "Let's see what this beauty can do."

She fired the weapon, and it produced a bolt of blue light that burned through Preedo's shoulder. The recoil sent her flying backward. As she recovered, she saw that the assault had only angered the scaly Nephilim, and he was upon her so swiftly, she didn't have time to aim again. He leapt forward and, with his good appendage, Preedo reached back and prepared to claw her face to ribbons.

One hell of a plan, Telkor, Camilla shielded herself and braced for the blow. *This thing is basically a goddamn dinosaur, so it's no wonder I couldn't wax him with one shot. Also, coulda warned me about the recoil on that spaced-out taser gun you gave me. Shit!*

The world around her slowed down to nearly a halt. Camilla shut her eyes and remembered the long dream she had during her time sealed in the cryo-bed. She saw the run-down pool hall in Southern Maryland where she'd spent her nights bartending, mopping up, or doing whatever odd jobs were needed to keep the doors open there. She remembered the pandemic that shuttered those doors despite her best efforts too. She hadn't seen a mirror since she'd left the tank, but she remembered her own face; the short chin, wide lips, and large eyes with pupils like anthracite suspended in white smoke. She recalled the beige of her palms of her umber hands and the faces they'd caressed.

In the brief moment it took for Preedo to close the distance between himself and her, Camilla clung to the moments that formed the life she had before she took a walk in a deserted wooded area near her home. There wasn't a soul outside then. Everyone had walled themselves inside away from the virus, and it had felt to Camille as if nature had exhaled as they did, letting herself thrive and bloom with little disruption. And Camille was drawn to it, the peace of it. One day she ventured further until she could hear the quiet trickle of a nearby stream and sat there until the yellow sky that canopied the trees melted into oranges, then blues. Finally, when she stood and dusted off her jeans, there was light pressing her in from all sides. Before she could determine the source of it, it had swallowed the world around her, this purgatorial chamber of white that stretched forever in every direction Camille turned. Then, hands on her body. Strange and coarse. Then, a coffin of water, or something that felt like water. And finally, a voice in the dark, speaking a language she could not understand. Then, pressure in her ear. A device that wrapped her mind around the warbled low notes of the tall, slender form pulling her from the darkness, warmth, and dreams of the liquid. A cloaked figure with scaly skin slipping its hand in hers, standing her up on wobbly legs, referring to her as "C6," and hastening her to run.

Camille rolled to the right just as Preedo's claws connected with her flesh, but his knife-like talons tore through her side like butter. She screamed but couldn't hear the sound exit her mouth. The pain had already congealed itself around her senses, and sights and sounds began to rapidly slip away. Then, consciousness itself.

"You...traitorous LIAR," Preedo growled. "I will inform Tower Nine immediately. You'll be exiled for this. No. No. No—that isn't enough; I'll see you burned for this!"

"Not if I don't burn you first," Telkor squared his stance and adjusted the recoil on the weapon with one fluid movement of his fingers, then fired it at Preedo's head.

The two mighty horns, the creased face, and the wide lipless mouth that concealed the two rows of deadly teeth, all of it disintegrated as he reached for the comms device in the pocket of Preedo's uniform cloak. Bits of him blanketed the small space, but Telkor had no time to clean it. He didn't wait to absorb what had gone wrong, record notes on those findings, or produce a report on the outcomes, as had been his routine for more Vaxxor sun-cycles than he could count. Instead, he scooped Camille, wrapped her in a spare uniform cloak, and boarded the auto-craft hovering outside his pod. Then, he keyed in coordinates he'd never used before in his life, and they began their descent into the Lowly Domes.

By the time they'd reached the bottom, the sounds and smells that Telkor knew best were gone, and the ones that replaced them wreaked turmoil on Telkor's gut, sparking hunger or nausea depending on the direction he took. Finally, he found what he was looking for.

That's the symbol, Telkor hoisted Camille from his shoulder to his arms and tapped on the door with his lengthy right foot. *Here goes.*

"We are up to code, Predictor," a shaky voice said just beyond the closed double doors.

"That is not why I'm here...now please, open the doors," Telkor was suddenly aware of his own tiredness, but he stood up straight and tried to look the part of a Vaxxor official when the doors slid open.

A squat, bluish Vaxxorian answered the door. He wore a

soiled apron and carried a surgical tool that looked awkwardly small in his left hand. Telkor's stomach churned when he laid eyes on him, as he looked similar to Preedo in many ways. But, the main difference that Telkor noted instantly was that when the Vaxxorian spoke, his face was closer to Telkor than his body. Telkor reasoned that it was because he likely tended toward quadrupedal movement, as he had heard many in the Lowly Domes did.

Guess it makes sense to want to move faster if you live down here, Telkor stepped back a little and shifted his weight from foot to foot, his arms burning with the weight of his bleeding cargo. *Still, his face is too close for comfort, really.*

"I'm Trimmux—let me help you with that," Trimmux swept Camille from Telkor's arms before he could object and waddled toward a stretcher in the middle of the large pod.

The room was dim but had high ceilings with a skylight at its top. The furniture was ergonomically suited from Trimmux's body; most seats looked to Telkor like massive, oblong bowls made low to the ground. In one, there was a throw pillow and a side table with a holoprojector pod on it, next to an empty, transparent tumbler full of dark liquid.

That must be his entertainment area, Telkor mused.

Telkor let his arms relax at his side and followed. He watched Trimmux carefully as he removed the blood-soaked uniform cloak from Camille's limp body.

"Is that…an Earthian?" Trimmux began. "Don't see many of those things down in the Domes."

"I found her this way and thought it my duty to bring her here for treatment, is all." Telkor smiled with only his mouth, and Trimmux waddled nervously toward a table full of tools and devices near an operating table. "Can you fix it or not?"

"Absolutely," Trimmux said merrily. "It's just a little blood loss. I can laser it and inject a few nanobots to take care of any remaining damage. Out of pain meds, though. Credits have been scarce this sun-cycle."

Well, I didn't have to be a Predictor to predict this, Telkor used a voice command to locate Trimmux's credit code in the database of his comms wristlet. He called it out, and Trimmux confirmed it with a nod. Then, Telkor transferred a substantial sum to the horned physician.

Trimmux had affixed a large, complex-looking helmet to his head during the few moments that Telkor had looked down at his comms wristlet, and it looked so outrageously silly to Telkor that he stifled a laugh when he looked up.

"How long will it be?" Telkor cleared his throat. "Meetings and such, you know."

"Of course, of course," Trimmux mumbled, already hard at work cleaning and repairing the wound, after which a robotic arm extending from the helmet sealed each completed portion closed. "Shouldn't be long at all."

Trimmux hummed as he worked, waddling a step or two to the left or right of Camille to ensure that each instrument protruding from his helmet could reach her wounds at the right angle. Telko rolled each eye in different directions in the room until he spotted a seat, then sank into it satisfactorily, sighing as he did. Afterward, Telkor sat up and realized that he had fallen asleep. He gasped and sprang to his feet.

How long was I unconscious? Telkor found the room empty and heard no voices. *Where are they? Have I been found out?*

Then he heard a low rumble of laughter coming from a curtain that Telkor suddenly realized was a partition and not decoration. He swept it back and found Trimmux and Camille seated, with empty plates in front of them.

"Well," Camille smiled, "Can't say I've ever had—what was it you called it, Trimmux?"

"Niarini," Trimmux answered gingerly.

"Niarini...but it wasn't half bad," Camille continued. "Then again, I've been tube-fed slop for the three years I was in that dream-box, so this was actually an—"

Trimmux froze.

Shit, Camille studied his face and calculated her misstep in their conversation. *You really suck at this quiet escapee thing, Camille.*

"Wh-what did you just say?!" Trimmux asked, his voice trembling. "Did you say you were in a 'Dream box'? Were you in a cryo-chamber? Are—are you the fugitive?!"

Telkor had his weapon drawn before Trimmu could access his comms wristlet.

"Listen to me, Trimmux," he said calmly. "We've both had a long day and have an appointment we need to keep. I've already sent you a generous portion of the units I'd stored up in preparation of this little excursion, and all I'm asking you to do is, let us leave quietly. Can you do that?"

Trimmux nodded and held his reptilian forelimbs out in front of him in a gesture of cooperation. With the weapon trained on Trimmux, Telkor snatched a handful of nearini and jammed it in the front pocket of his cloak, then reached for Camille with the other hand. Together, they backed away slowly. When they'd reached the entrance, Telkor found that it opened with a simple lever switch and not the complex biometric system like the pods in the upper domes. Just as they were about to cross the threshold, they overheard Trimmux relaying a frantic message through his comms wristlet. Suddenly, Camille snatched her elbow away from Telkor and ran to the center of the room.

"What in the two suns are you doing?!" Telkor spun around and saw that Camille was searching for something in the corner of the room.

"Got it!" Camille held up the helmet Trimmux had used to treat her wounds earlier. "I have a feeling I might need this later...especially since he divulged that this thing basically does all the work."

She ran back to Telkor's side, and in a breath, they thrust themselves back into the sights and sounds of the Lowly Domes. They ran behind a transparent navigation screen that Telkor was projecting from his comms wristlet, and to Camille, it felt like chasing a square blue ghost until her sides burned. Her short legs struggled to keep pace with Telkor's lanky ones, and after several turns in which she nearly plowed into beings who looked to her like lizard dogs, salamander-faced humanoids like Telkor, and small, winged dinosaurs, she doubled over and motioned for Telkor to stop.

They had been running nonstop, and when Telkor slowed to allow them to rest, both slowly absorbed the notion that the Lowly Domes was less colorful and benign in the dark. Telkor wasn't accustomed to the winged creatures and winced every time one swooped past his head. More unnerving was that they discovered that the translators in their ears were starting to glitch. The Lowly Domes had their own dialects, and some of it was spoken so fast that it became guttural gibberish in their ears the closer they got to their destination.

"Are we almost there?" Camille asked after she caught her breath and stood up straight again. "Not that I have any idea where we're going in the first place."

"Luckily," Telkor managed his words between mouthfuls

of niarini, "we're nearly there. All we need to do is—"

The blast of light stung both their eyes, and it came from directly above. After adjusting to the indigo hue of dim pod lights and moving swiftly with their heads down as they walked, Telkor and Camille had felt somewhat secure in their journey. Now, as they looked around them, squinting at the buildings that flanked them on all sides, they quickly figured out what they should have been paying more attention to all along.

Shit...our goddamn faces are everywhere, Camille's stomach churned as she looked around.

Several digital billboards displayed images of her and Telkor. In the broadcast, images of Telkor showed him receiving awards, standing next to what Camille guessed were other Vaxxorian officials, and delivering what appeared to be a heartfelt speech at a podium. The next clip showed Preedo's body being transported from Telkor's now ransacked pod. Then, the last part of the broadcast showed a clip of Camille in the only bar fight she'd ever been in. In it, Camille was wearing a white tank and jeans and brandishing a pool stick as a weapon against a burly, tattooed man in her former workplace. Customers scurried for the exit as she swept the man's feet from under him with the pool stick, broke a bottle against the bar, and straddled the man to the floor with the jagged glass pressed against the man's temple drawing blood. Her locs hung in her face as she threatened the man into submission before rising and kicking him in his side as she walked away.

Oh, this is clearly some bull shit, Camille's mouth hung open in awe. *I see they're not gonna run the part about the guy being a Nazi piece of shit. How did they even find this? But I guess I shouldn't be surprised.*

The rest of the broadcast profiled Camille as a dangerous Earthian escapee called "C6" and warned Vaxxorians about the carnage she'd left in her wake. It ended with a voiceover advising residents that she had likely taken a Predictor named Telkor hostage after killing his associate, Preedo.

Telkor looked at her, and Camille nodded knowingly. Then, they ran. Telkor had turned his comms wristlet off as they watched the broadcast, so they ran without direction, focused only on finding a pocket of darkness to hide from the floodlights of the craft hovering overhead. After what seemed like a never-ending sprint, they both determined that fleeing was useless.

"This is where the Lower Domes end, so it's not like we've got anywhere else to run anyway," Telkor panted out the somber words.

"Wait—these are actual domes down here?" Camille sputtered, out of breath. "This whole damn alien ghetto is inside a dome? How'd I miss that?"

They looked around and noticed that the floodlights had dimmed, but they could still hear the hum of the menacing craft nearby.

"Well, you were unconscious for the ride down," Telkor shrugged. "But yeah, I had to leave my craft at a hub so that we could take the tube-ride down—that's why I don't have it now."

"So, what you're saying is, we've got no ride outta here?" Camille's shoulders slumped under the realization, and her resolve evaporated.

"That's right," a voice to their right called out. "You do not."

Camille's eyes burned with sweat, and she could only make out the outline of the person approaching them. The form was tall and lean, with an oblong head and lengthy hands and feet. It walked with a pendulous rhythm and had several weapons holstered on its waist and one on its ankle.

"Unless...you come with me," the Vaxxorian finished.

"Camille, meet Porma," Telkor gestured as he bowed.

"No time for that bowing nonsense," Porma's calm, regal tone fell away as she fumed. "Why did you make me chase you all the way here?"

The two continued to argue, and Camille watched them for a moment, her eyes darting back and forth between the pair. Then, she unzipped her wetsuit to the chest and rolled up her sleeves. She crouched down to place the helmet she'd stolen from Trimmux on the ground and removed a sharp tool from the end of one of its robotic arms. She used it to saw through one dense loc, then another, until most of her hair lay in severed rope-like fragments near her feet. Then, she began walking toward the direction Porma had emerged from.

"How was I to know you'd commandeer an official government craft for this?" Telkor folded his arms across his chest, continuing to argue.

"You know full well that it's the only kind that is permitted down here—did you expect me to take a civilian craft into an airspace with no other civilian crafts?" Porma snapped. "We would have been found out by sunset if I didn't make it look like a recovery operation of some sort."

At that, Porma turned away from Telkor abruptly and began walking behind Camille. Telkor stood gawking indignantly for a moment, then trotted to catch up. Once they had boarded and performed a series of checks, Camille guided the craft upward, then further upward still. After the craft had crossed a narrow entry reserved for law enforcement and rescue service crafts, Camille landed the craft, which was scarcely the size of Telkor's pod, and gathered her effects.

"You're sure you won't come?" Telkor beseeched his longtime companion once more as she exited the craft.

"I will not," Porma said coolly, then, turning to Camille. "Have you any idea what it means to couple with a being so predictable, he is referred to as 'The Predictor'?"

"Can't say that I do," Camille answered apprehensively.

"Well, it's a long journey back to wherever you're from, so you're about to find out," Porma quipped. Telkor rolled both eyes away from the conversation as she continued. "Be safe, both of you, and I bid you the blessings of Vaxxor's Twin Suns. Goodbye."

And with that, Porma turned and slinked away. Watching her go, Camille could not help but admire her directness and air of indifference. She decided that she liked her, even if she'd never see her again.

The airlock sealed with a thud, followed by a hydraulic hiss and a computerized voice stating that the craft had repressurized.

Telkor surveyed each corner of the craft, then pulled up several holoprojections to check the inventory of their vital resources, engine systems, and navigation. Once satisfied, he seated himself where Porma had previously been seated, and Camille shifted to his previous seat, next to it.

"Are we headed back to Earth?" Camille raised an eyebrow.

"That depends—how well can you swim?" Telkor avoided eye contact as he replied.

"It's that bad, huh?" Camille's heart pounded.

Has everything been wiped out? Where will I go? How will I—

"You're not the only Earthian I've smuggled out,

Camille," Telkor said quietly.

"What? Where are the others, and why didn't it go more smoothly?" Camille probed Telkor as he busied himself with inputting coordinates into the craft's navigation."

"I tampered with the read-outs and had some of the specimens presumed dead, then I smuggled them away from the breeding program through a network of other officials who feel the way that I now do," Telkor finally turned toward Camille. "Porma was one of those officials. She works closely with the elite at Tower Nine and is tied into the Vaxxorian breeding program in many ways. My job as Predictor was to determine which lifeforms were optimal for breeding, and Porma's official title used to be 'Selector.' She was tasked with scrutinizing large batches of those selections and presenting a final list to our extraction teams.

"After many sun cycles," Telkor continued, "the process began to wear Porma down. It may be that, because we have been intermingling with Earthians and other specimens who tend toward familial ties, we have developed some of the same sensibilities; I cannot say. Porma and I both used The Collector, a machine that creates visualizations of selectees' memories while they are in cryosleep, and the things we saw, especially from Earthians, sometimes terrified us. All I'm certain of is that, eventually, Porma became more careful and began to only select Earthians with no families and those who were not engaged in long-term coupling."

"So, really, what you're saying is...I was chosen because I was alone, and now I may end up alone forever because of that?" Camille sighed and fastened her restraints.

"You won't end up alone," Telkor's hands were a blur on the controls as he continued. "There's a planet in an area Earthians refer to as 'Alpha Centauri,' and it's much like Earth. It's a bit bigger and colder, but refugees are faring well there, per the last report I read. Also, we did not select you based on your solitude. We selected you, and The Collector confirmed you as a viable candidate because your age, lineage, genes, and physical traits were favorable not only for breeding but also suited to survive a rescue mission and transport."

After some hydraulic hissing and rumbling of the craft, Vaxxor began to shrink beneath them.

"I see," Camille said as she looked out onto the black highway before them, paved with celestial bodies and pebbled with stars, pensively.

She considered her deep brown skin, mesomorphic body type, and hair that coiled close to her scalp, warding off all styles except the locs that formed when she rolled its kinky sections between her fingers. She considered the noise of the bar, the stack of bills that had accumulated on the wobbly kitchen table of her dilapidated home in Clinton, Maryland. The love that escaped her, time and time again, like fistfuls of sand. She tallied twenty-nine Earth years filled with disappointment, hardship, and unappreciation and weighed it all against what Telkor was telling her at that moment—that she was handpicked as an optimal choice. Then, as she looked out at the night, unrolling itself for a million miles in every direction, she remembered the peace of the creek near her home and discovered that this view brought her that same peace.

"Okay, then. I'm headed somewhere new, and I guess I'm okay with that, but you still left out the part about why my rescue mission was so different," Camille's glimmer of a brief smile morphed into a frown. "I fucked it up, didn't I?"

Telkor chuckled. It was a throaty, whirry sound that Camille couldn't quite quantify because she had never heard anything like it.

"You did 'fuck it up, but that is not why," Telkor continued when his laughter had subsided. "This mission is different because I am not returning to Vaxxor. I had been planning to leave for some time, but I suppose Preedo's death did force my hand a bit."

Now that they were away from the planet, Camille saw Vaxxor for the first time. It looked smaller than Earth, and its atmosphere was a patchwork of deep yellows, blues, and grays that melted into one another the higher their craft ascended.

"So," Camille said cheerfully, looking around at her new

home for the long journey. "New rules. First, I hear all you talkin'...but don't think you're gonna dump me on some planet where I'll be picking alien cotton and having massa's pale green babies. I don't think I need to remind you about the last wave of Earthians who looked like me and were abducted for their physical traits—do I?"

"No, you don't," Telkor shuddered and grimaced, and Camille smiled at the reaction.

"Second thing is, if we're gonna be stuck in this flying luxury suite for the next few months or 'sun cycles'—as you Vaxxorians put it—then I need to know why you left, Telkor. I want the truth."

In the few moments of silence that passed between them, Telkor trained his eyes on his home planet, observing it quietly and for what he predicted would be his last time.

"I'm leaving because I have seen what it is for a species to accomplish so much that it devours itself through thrill-seeking, pomp, and indifference," Telkor said, his eyes still glued on the shrinking sphere of yellow, blue, and gray. "I've witnessed the growing divide between those who closely serve the powerful Vaxxorians in Tower Nine—walking upright in our decorated cloaks—and the squalor and futility of life in the Lower Domes, which I had begun to ridicule as 'lowly' or somehow lowlier than my own life. In short, I have seen what happens when, under a veil of order, a species becomes as chaotic as they are bored. I've seen it in The Collector, in Porma's weary eyes, and my own. I've seen it, and now I believe it is time for me to see something else; time for me to be something else."

"Damn, Telkor," Camille leaned back and interlaced her fingers behind her head. "I couldn't have said it better myself."